THE SUDDEN
DISAPPEARANCE
OF THE WORKER BEES

THE SUDDEN DISAPPEARANCE OF THE WORKER BEES

A Commissario Simona Tavianello Mystery

SERGE QUADRUPPANI

Translated from the Italian
by Delia Casa

Arcade Publishing • New York

First Arcade Paperback Edition 2015

Arcade Publishing books may be purchased in bulk at special discounts for
sales promotion, corporate gifts, fund-raising, or educational purposes. Special
editions can also be created to specifications. For details, contact the Special Sales
Department, Arcade Publishing, 307 West 36th Street, 11th Floor, New York, NY
10018 or arcade@skyhorsepublishing.com.

Arcade Publishing® is a registered trademark of Skyhorse Publishing, Inc.®, a
Delaware corporation.

Visit our website at www.arcadepub.com.

10 9 8 7 6 5 4 3 2 1

Library of Congress Cataloging-in-Publication Data is available on file.

Cover design by Georgia Morrissey

Print ISBN: 978-1-62872-528-5
Ebook ISBN: 978-1-61145-941-8

Printed in the United States of America

CHAPTER 1

"ARE YOU GOING TO TELL ME WHY YOU'RE SULKING?"

"I'm not sulking. I'm annoyed."

"Ah, and what's the difference?"

"Sulking means putting on a disagreeable expression and not talking. I, on the other hand, am perfectly willing to explain any annoyance I may express."

Commissario Simona Tavianello took her eyes off the mountain road they were driving on to observe her husband, retired police chief Marco Tavianello, his face in profile. The thin wrinkles at the corners of his light blue eyes were more accentuated than usual, the rim of his lower lip protruding and tensed. No doubt about it—he was sulking. What's more, his answer demonstrated a strongly contentious attitude. She sighed and redirected her attention to the approaching turn in the road, a tight curve flanked by

1

long-branched, visibility-reducing Douglas pines. When she had gotten past it, she asked:

"Fine, so are you going to tell me why you're ticked off?"

"I'm sick of you always throwing your bag in my lap when you're driving. I've told you a thousand times that it hurts. And it makes me look like a dick."

Simona glanced at the rearview mirror, then huffed:

"Is that all? Is that why you've been sulking since we left the hotel?"

"I'm sick of you always racing straight ahead, eyes on the road in front of you, never taking my feelings into account."

"On this, the first real morning of spring, with the sun shining and not a cloud in the sky after the eight days of rain that effectively ruined the first week of my vacation, *il signore* decides to sulk, deforming his expertly seductive mouth, all because I set my bag down on his muscular thighs and he finds it emasculating?"

"Don't act like you don't know what I'm talking about. It's thoughtless on your part. You don't want to put your bag on the floor, apparently because you don't want to get it dirty. And you know perfectly well that I get a pain in my shoulders every time I have to turn around to put it on the backseat. On top of that, no sooner do I set it down than I hear something ringing inside and I've got to pick it up again to fish around for a cell phone that stops ringing the second I find it."

"So basically you're saying that life with me is hell, and after thirty years you've decided to fight back?"

As she said this she had started to slow down; they had reached a driveway, at the end of which stood a one-story house made of wood, its roof blanketed with flowering vegetation. As she maneuvered around the sandy terrain where some slabs of slate marked a parking spot, he retorted:

"You're making fun of me so you don't have to respond."

"Respond to what?" she asked, retrieving a large ethnic bag overflowing with countless objects from her husband's lap. "Respond to the accusation that I don't take your feelings into account? Why do you think we're here anyway?"

She pointed to the sign in front of which she had parked: MINONCELLI: HONEY, HONEY DESSERTS, POLLEN, HONEY ESSENCES, MOUNTAIN PLANTS.

"Oh, you're so full of it . . . You're the one who suggested it this morning!" Marco erupted as he opened the door. "You wanted to spend our last morning buying honey instead of taking a walk."

"You're the one who's full of it!" rejoined Simona, slamming the car door and locking it. "You've been saying that you wanted to buy honey for days, and we've either got to do it now or we're not doing it at all. Let me remind you that we came to Piedmont because *il signore* prefers the mountains to the sea, whereas I would've rather spent my entire vacation in the Aeolian Islands."

"Oh, you'll be in the Aeolian Islands tomorrow anyway. And I know someone who will be happy to see you."

"What are you talking about?"

"Come on, don't play dumb. You know perfectly well what I mean . . . What's his name, the owner of the *pension* . . . Michele?"

"Yeah, Michele. So?"

"You think I didn't see him drooling over you when you were tanning by the pool last year?"

Simona burst out laughing and shook her head, hurrying to catch up with her husband as he walked swiftly in the direction of the cabin.

"I can't believe this!" she exclaimed at Marco's back, which remained in front of her, rigid in his linen suit. "Now you're putting on a jealous-husband act for me? What's going on? Did you sleep badly?"

Three steps led up to a wooden terrace, which time and the weather had turned gray. As he climbed the steps one by one, she caught up to him with a hop and grabbed him by the arm. He turned around. "Are you being serious?" she pressed.

And seeing that the masculine face maintained its stony expression, she assumed a gentler tone.

"Come on, Marco, have you seen me? I'm fifty-seven years old and twenty pounds overweight."

"So what? You're still very attractive. And that pig fat you were smearing on yourself made your tits glow. And you're right, I didn't sleep well, because this is what I was dreaming about last night. I know, it's ridiculous—it was a year ago. But it still pisses me off."

With one hand Simona brushed a wisp of her bountiful ivory-colored hair out of her eyes, and with the other she took Marco's neck.

"Kiss me," she said, trying to draw him toward her. "You haven't kissed me yet today."

"Stop it," he said, resisting, but with his lips folded in a smile that brought the light back to his face. "What will people think . . . two old people kissing?"

In one fluid and sprightly motion, she positioned herself at his side, pushed him with her shoulder, and walked toward the door.

"*You're* the old one!" she said.

She paused on the threshold of the wood-and-mortar building, with its narrow, double-paned windows, the scent of hay and flowers wafting down from the roof. The door was just slightly ajar.

"Are you sure it's not too early?" Marco asked her from behind.

"Too early? It's almost ten. And let's get one thing straight," she added with a decisive tone. "If you want to have a good time today, you'd better get it into your head that I've had enough of you talking about our ages. Yours *and* mine."

Marco sighed.

"Fine, but to return to the subject at hand: maybe it's nine, maybe it's not. If you hadn't been in such a rush to leave, I would've gone back up to our room to get my watch and my phone, and right now we'd know exactly what time it is. But you've always got to be the boss."

Simona knocked loudly on the door, waited a few moments, then opened it.

"Is anyone home?"

When no one answered, she gave the door another push—but something kept her from opening it all the way.

"What are you doing?" Marco asked at her back. "Wait a second . . ."

But she had already stepped inside.

"Wait." Marco sighed again. "You always have to rush in. Instead of simplifying things, you make them more complicated . . ."

"Marco." Simona turned to face him. "There's a body on the ground."

"Right," Marco said. "That's exactly what I'm talking about."

"A man with a hole in his head."

"Right," Marco repeated. "That's all we need right now." It was the voice of a man who had given up.

* * *

Iris, bellflower, honeysuckle, daisies . . .

As Maresciallo Calabonda finished taking down Marco's observations in a notebook—she had let him lead the investigation from the moment they discovered the body—Simona was reading from the informational poster stuck to one of the beams overhead, directly above the long wooden table where they were seated in the rear of the house. The text explained the benefits of a "flowering roof" and listed the varieties of wildflower present on the roof of the cottage. A fragrant breeze from above carried with it a faint, constant buzzing—a noise that they hadn't detected as they approached the house upwind. From where they were sitting they could make out a field that sloped up gently for about a hundred yards to reach the foot of a pine forest, where dozens of man-made beehives were arranged side by side. It seemed the bees preferred the orchids that proliferated on the roof of the house belonging to Giovanni Minoncelli, the beekeeper.

"No, this man is not Giovanni," the maresciallo responded to one of Marco's questions. "I know him. I've dealt with him more than once."

"You mean he's run into trouble before?"

"He's a militant environmentalist. A leader. We've picked him up for unlawful occupation of property, unauthorized demonstrations, obstructing traffic . . . basically your first-rate pain in the ass. He'll have to explain why there's a dead body behind his door when we bring him in."

The maresciallo closed his notebook, tucked it away in a worn leather briefcase, and peered at his two interlocutors through his sunglasses, which, along with his cap, his tanned skin, and his dark mustache, made him look like he had just stepped out of an army recruitment poster.

"To sum things up, when you discovered the body, the only thing you did was to enter and make a telephone call, because neither one of you had your cell phone. You walked to the telephone; you picked it up, holding the handset with a tissue, and you returned outside to wait for us; and during this time, your wife remained outside. Is that correct?"

"Correct."

"Good. Thank you, Chief. Really. You made every effort not to alter the crime scene. But of course coming from you that does not surprise me. It is a pleasure and an honor to work with such a true professional. I am sorry that your vacation has been ruined by a trivial piece of rural crime."

"Where murder is concerned, the crime is never trivial."

The maresciallo ran a hand over his mustache with an expression that was difficult to interpret.

"You're right," he said. "One last question . . . Did you notice anything on the table when you made the phone call?"

Marco furrowed his brow. Several seconds passed. He shook his head.

"No. There was a pile of papers scattered on the table but I didn't look at them closely. As I told you, I did not try to examine the scene. It was not my place to do so."

Calabonda pulled a transparent plastic envelope out of his briefcase and showed it to Marco. It contained a single sheet of paper and bore an official seal.

"You didn't notice this sheet of paper on the table?"

The police chief stared at the evidence. There were four words on the page, written in marker in large letters: THE WORKER BEE REVOLUTION. He shook his head.

"No."

Calabonda sighed, returning the envelope to his briefcase.

"We found it three feet from the body," he explained. "Seeing as a window was open and there was a good breeze, what I would really like to know is whether this sheet of paper was originally on the table or on the body. In the latter case, it could be a sort of claim of responsibility."

Marco nodded.

"And Signora . . . Commissario. I take it you didn't notice this paper when you pushed the door open?" Calabonda asked Simona.

Torn from her contemplation of the mountain pastures—the rays of the sun, which had suddenly risen from behind the peak, had enveloped the fields in a golden fog—the commissario said in a whisper:

"No, I didn't see it. But, as we've already explained to you, sir, I went back outside immediately. I didn't have time to see what lay around the body."

"Well, thank you," the maresciallo said, standing with his hands resting on the wooden table. "I'll get in touch with you at the Hôtel des Roches before your departure," he made clear as he got out of the chair sideways, one leg at a time. "You'll be here for another week, is that right?"

"Yes, at the very most," Simona said, as her face entered the crosshairs of a gun sight.

The maresciallo got to his feet and his face in turn entered the crosshairs, his temple positioned right at the intersection of the two lines at the center of the circle.

Marco stood up as well, and his profile joined the maresciallo's in the scope as he extended his hand for a shake.

So the two officers went to retrieve their vehicle and the maresciallo went to talk to the head of Forensics, who had men in white jumpsuits combing the house for evidence. The camouflaged man who had captured each of the three law enforcers' heads in his gun sight brushed off the pine needles that had stuck to his jumpsuit, slung the gun over his shoulder, and disappeared into the darkness of the forest.

*   *   *

A half hour later on the terrace of the Hôtel des Roches, against a backdrop of steep slopes, trails of mud and debris, waterfalls, and towering rocks that alternated sharply with rounded, grass-covered ones, Giuseppe Felice, a local reporter with fire-red hair, ordered a second cappuccino that he had no interest in drinking. For him it was only a matter of waiting for the right moment to stand up and

make his way across the terrace, weaving between the pine-
wood tables where families in brightly colored clothes sat
noisily consuming their breakfasts, to the spot where a
tanned and elegant sixty-something man and a white-haired
woman were having an animated discussion. He waited,
because as soon as he had gotten close enough he would
have to ask whether Signore and Signora Tavianello would
perhaps consider honoring him with an exclusive interview
for his newspaper, *Il Quotidiano delle Valli*. He waited, that
is, because Giuseppe Felice suffered from an extremely
unpleasant condition for a reporter: he was shy.

The truth is that he didn't have any trouble when it
came to interviewing one of the small-time valley business-
men who made their fortunes by having undocumented
immigrants work ten hours a day to produce shoes or
metal parts, and whose sons got their kicks driving around
in their SUVs and harassing those very same immigrants
by night. All he had to do was turn on the tape recorder and
then transcribe their monologues on the virtues of their
own companies and of the Northern League, the right-
wing political party known for its conservative stance on
immigration, among other things.

This defect was even less of an issue when he was
performing his usual work of transcribing the press
releases of local politicians—adjusting a comma here
and there—and reporting on the town festivals and folk
celebrations, marriages and births among the local nota-
bles, and hunters' association gatherings. But when it

happened that a national celebrity passed through San Giorgio al Monte and the editor in chief, the honorable Dottore Signorelli, called him up demanding that he get an exclusive interview—those were, as they say in Italian, bitter cabbages, and he just had to grin and bear it.

Nevertheless, he knew how to arrange these meetings perfectly. Giuseppe Felice had gifts unknown to his employer, gifts that, in another corner of the world and with the right contacts, would have allowed him to add a few zeros to his pitiful monthly salary. Among these gifts was his ability to unearth a startling amount of information online, even breaching network security if necessary. But he didn't have to dig deep to find information on the couple who had discovered the body of an unidentified man at Minoncelli's house. A simple Internet search returned 420,000 results for Simona Tavianello and 372,000 for her husband. The higher number of hits for the woman was surely due to the fact that she worked for the National Antimafia Commission and had participated in various media investigations, which had resulted in numerous invitations to academic conferences. Marco Tavianello had also had a brilliant career—though more low-key—in the fight against drug trafficking. Many members of the press had made malicious comments with regard to his early retirement, seeing it as evidence of his doubts about the political influences operating in his field. But the former police chief had not expressed himself in this regard, as he was generally very reluctant to be interviewed.

Giuseppe Felice set his cup down as though he had realized in a flash how perverse it was to put milk in coffee, since it denatured the taste and rendered it indigestible. He remembered the day that, hoping to interview a famous Italian actress known for playing neurotic, middle-bourgeois characters, he had hesitated so long and so nervously broken with his natural shyness that he ended up spilling a glass of highly tannic—and therefore particularly red—valley wine all over the signora's elegant and expensive dress.

Maybe I should wait until the wife is alone to approach her, he thought to himself. *That way she'll be more willing to give an interview.* But no; Signorelli had insisted: "I want both of them—it'll be a story that'll run nationwide, I'm sure of it." *Fine*, he thought, *I'll get up, I'll walk over to them, and I'll ask, boldly yet politely, if they might grant me a few minutes of their time for an interview. Let's go, getting up now . . .* he repeated to himself, without moving a muscle. Then he averted his gaze, because the commissario was staring back at him.

"Have you seen that guy who's been eyeing us for a while?" Simona was saying to Marco. "How much you want to bet that he's from the Services—a regional security agent?"

"Aren't you being a little paranoid?" Marco replied.

"What, you think this story hasn't gotten the Services' attention? A guy's body is found at the home of an ecologist along with a signature that says 'The Worker Bee Revolution,' and you think they're not going to do anything?"

"For starters, we don't know for sure that it is a signature."

"You know very well that it is," the commissario responded, lowering her voice. "When we entered, the sheet of paper was on the body—"

"What? What are you talking about?"

"Yes, now that I think about it, I'm almost certain that I perceived . . . like a movement, something white moving next to the body when I stepped inside. I must have created a slight current of air that moved the sheet of paper away from it . . ."

From the other side of the terrace, Felice observed the chief's bewildered expression.

"Why didn't you say anything before?"

"Because it's a detail that just came to me now," Simona said with conviction. Then she shook her head. "But it could be a posteriori autosuggestion . . . I don't know."

"Fine, forget it," Marco said seriously. "That Calabonda seems entirely competent to me, and it's vital that our presence here not disturb him. I can already see all of the psychological complications—the policeman from a Podunk provincial town under the microscope of two big shots from Rome. The more we keep our distance the better it will be for everyone involved. We're on vacation, and we've done our civic duty. There's no reason for us to get mixed up in this case any more than we already have," he concluded as he prepared to answer his phone, which was ringing.

Seeing Marco with his cell phone glued to his ear, Giuseppe Felice told himself that the right moment had arrived. The couple's conversation had been interrupted, and he'd be able to introduce himself as soon as the retired police chief's phone call was finished.

"This is Maresciallo Calabonda," the carabiniere said into Marco's ear. "I need to meet with your wife right away."

Marco frowned. *Fuck*, he thought. *He must have found out that the paper was on the body somehow, and he wants to know how she failed to notice it.*

"You want to see Simona?" Marco asked, directing a grimace at the woman in question. "May I ask why?"

"You know that I'm not obliged to answer that."

"That's quite right, my friend and colleague. You're not," Marco conceded in a tone that was neutral enough to imply a threat.

Calabonda let out an exasperated sigh, then said all in one breath:

"She needs to explain how the bullet found in the head of the victim—who we've identified, by the way— how it's possible that the gun from which this bullet was fired, according to the serial number, belongs to your wife."

Good, Felice thought as he watched the couple exchange puzzled and anxious words and gestures. *Now I can head over there, before they get up—plus, it looks like there's news.*

Come on, go! he ordered himself again as the two police officials got to their feet. *I'm going, I'm going,* he repeated to himself as they made their way toward the stairs that led to the hotel rooms. And he sat there, not moving an inch.

CHAPTER 2

*A*BOUT THIRTY MILES AS THE CROW flies from the
police compound where Maresciallo Calabonda was sitting down with Simona and Marco Tavianello, Giovanni
Minoncelli exited the Claudiana di Torre Pellice bookstore. Beyond the mountaintops whose peaks were still
covered with unmelted snow—snow in which all of the
valley's toxic emissions, including bromate-based fire-
proofing products, plasticizers containing phthalic acid,
and other persistent organic pollutants, were stored—
he walked across Piazza della Libertà, went back up Via
Mazzini, and turned onto Via Falchi. Beyond the chaos
of the rocks, icy streams, and mountain pastures from
which cows looked down on the world with their sweet,
fly-encircled, melancholy gazes, Minoncelli reached a
group of ten or so people standing in front of an excellent wine shop. Most of them were men and women in

their fifties. The majority of the men had beards, a handful of young people, including two pretty girls, sported various piercings, and they were all wearing bright colors and hiking shoes. The muscular Minoncelli, with curly blond hair and light blue eyes that stood out in his tan, handsome face, towered over all of them.

"Everything OK?" he inquired in his deep, gravelly smoker's voice. "Was anyone followed? Did everyone remove the batteries from their cell phones before leaving the house?"

Nods of assent. Stiff smiles. One could sense a certain tension among the members of the group.

"Let's get moving," said the beekeeper. "Quickly."

The party set off on foot, overtaking the sidewalk and spilling out into the street. But in that quiet hour of the morning, all that they encountered was a single car and one elderly woman being dragged along by her dog. The dog watched the small, silent, determined group in bewilderment, as its owner patiently waited for the animal to recommence yanking her forward. When they had passed the tall beige façade of the fortress of the Order of Saint Maurice, the little group turned onto a steep road and stopped in front of the gate of a villa. On the ground floor, wisteria heaped on top of a lattice sweetened the air all the way down to the street. In the outer wall next to the gate there was a little metal door. Minoncelli turned the handle and pushed, but the door resisted. A cluster of keys appeared in his hand; he stuck one in the keyhole and opened the door. Within a minute the little group was in the yard, and within two minutes they were inside the house. An alarm went off, but it stopped when someone cut a wire. On the second-floor balcony, above the lattice roof, a young woman and a scruffy young man put up a banner that read: WE'RE TAKING YOU OVER BECAUSE YOU'VE TAKEN OVER OUR LIVES. SACROPIANO = POISONER. SAVE THE BEES. And in smaller letters: ALPINE VALLEY BEEKEEPERS' DEFENSE LEAGUE.

In the large kitchen, a girl with various piercings opened the door of the enormous refrigerator, wondering if the instructions they'd been given to cause as little damage as possible applied to the food as well. She'd skipped breakfast and her stomach was growling, but she decided to restrain herself. As she walked back into the living room, where the owner's taste for African art and textiles was readily apparent, she was relieved to see that someone had pulled a thermos full of coffee and some packets of cookies out of a backpack. Several bottles of water were also making the rounds from one corner of the room to the other, where each member of the group had claimed a seat among the rhinoceros-skin couches, armchairs upholstered in tan-colored fabrics bearing sketches of lions and gazelles, and sub-Saharan rugs. They all kept their voices down as Minoncelli, the only one still on his feet, returned the battery to his cell phone, put the SIM card in place, waited for the little device to restart, and dialed a number. The voices went silent when he said, "Fuck." He looked up. "Felice's phone went straight to voice mail, even though I told him we were going to make a move this morning." Then he spoke into the phone: "Hello, Felice. This is Minoncelli. Right now our group is setting up to occupy the residence of Bertolazzi, the engineer, Sacropiano's regional manager in Piedmont. We've decided to boycott his press conference in Turin and have come to deliver our message to him at his home, just as Sacropiano comes to our homes to kill our bees. We're also going to alert the national media, so if you want an exclusive, move your ass."

He ended the call and barked, "Let's go! Now we're going to call the others."

Six activists who had also restarted their cell phones joined him in calling Rai3, Televalli, and the other television networks, along with the Turin offices of every major daily newspaper and various news agencies. When they'd finished, there was a brief silence. A broad smile spread across Minoncelli's horselike face.

"Good. Now I'll have the pleasure of alerting Calabonda."

He pulled the number up in his phone, dialed, and waited.

"He's not answering his phone and there's no voice mail set up. I'll call the barracks."

He redialed and spoke with someone at the main switchboard.

"He's busy? Tell him the call is from Minoncelli . . . Yes, this is him . . ." The beekeeper shot a sneer at his companions. "Guess my name opens a lot of doors down at police headquarters! . . . Yes, this is him. Yes. Turn myself in? Oh, definitely not, not right away, I assure you. No, I know what I'm saying. No, our group is occupying the home of Bertolazzi, the engineer, an associate of . . . what? Wait, what do you mean? No . . . no. No! Well, I'm obviously not up to speed—"

Minoncelli had gone pale. The others watched, aware that something unexpected had happened, something that would undoubtedly interfere with the usual series of events: the police siege of the occupied property; the media statement; the rigorous questioning; the imprisonment; the arraignment; the prisoner's release to the cheers of his companions; preparation for and media coverage of the upcoming trial.

"Yes, OK," Minoncelli said. "Of course I'll come. There's no point sending your thugs for me. Ah, yes, OK. OK. OK."

With every "OK" that Minoncelli directed at Maresciallo Calabonda, a whisper went up among the bee-defending comrades. They exchanged glances. When the conversation ended, a silence as heavy as lead fell over the room. A siren could be heard in the distance.

"The carabinieri are coming for me," he said at last. "I'm . . . they found a body at my house. They've identified it. It's Bertolazzi."

There was a moment of stunned silence. Then a heavyset forty-something woman managed to say:

"Bertolazzi's body, at your house? How is that possible? Wasn't he supposed to be at the press conference?" Minoncelli shook his head.

"He was supposed to be, yes, but—well, I've told you everything that Calabonda told me. That's all I know."

"But how did he die?" asked a bald man with a beard. "And at your house?"

"I don't know anything, I told you," Minoncelli repeated, looking back at him with fear in his eyes. "I don't know how he died, and I don't know how he ended up at my house."

The sound of the siren got so loud that the police car seemed to be there in the room with them.

* * *

Extremely tall, thin as a rail, with a head too small for his lanky body, hollow cheeks hidden behind a beard, and tousled hair, Daniele Evangelisti looked like he was better suited to act in B-movies than to practice law. He ended the phone call and smirked in the direction of the Tavianellos, who sat on the other side of his desk.

"That was Calabonda. He told me he found Minoncelli—or rather, Minoncelli called him to let him know that he and his accomplices had occupied Bertolazzi's villa in Torre Pellice. In other words, forty miles from here."

"Which could mean that he wasn't involved in the murder," Simona suggested.

The attorney lifted his long hands with the palms facing outward, then let them fall back into place, flat on the desk. The commissario found them attractive.

"It's possible," he said. "But to return to the theft of your gun, Signora Commissario: you maintain that you took every necessary precaution and observed every regulation in place?"

Simona sighed.

"Yes. As I just explained to you, I'm required to carry a personal firearm at all times, both on account of my professional duties and because I've led several investigations on behalf of the National Antimafia Agency. I'd locked it up in a little lockbox, thinking there was no chance of running into any danger around here . . ."

"And unfortunately, your impression was incorrect," the attorney said. "As you can see, we have our share of crime here as well. Do you have any idea when the theft of the weapon could have occurred?"

"As I told you, last night the lockbox was intact. It was only after Calabonda's phone call that we returned to our room to find that it had been broken into."

"So this puts us at what time, roughly?"

Simona shot a look at Marco, sitting rigidly in the chair next to hers. He shrugged. Those who knew him could have interpreted this to mean either "You're going to have to answer that one yourself," or "This thing is starting to drag on. When can we go eat?"

"This morning we went out early, around seven thirty, to go for a walk along the river. After eating breakfast around nine thirty we got into our car to go to Minoncelli's. If we take into account the time the murderer would have needed to get to Minoncelli's house and kill Bertolazzi, I'd say he probably stole the gun between seven thirty and nine at the latest. Maybe he was watching us and entered our room right after we left. It didn't look to me like the door had been forced, but that kind of lock isn't difficult to get open . . ."

Marco scowled at Simona. He knew that tone well, recognized the intensity with which his wife spoke those words. It was painfully clear that she was starting to become invested in the case. Not good. He decided to intervene.

"I suppose it would be best for us to stay away from our room as long as is necessary for Forensics to complete their survey. We'll leave it to you for the entire day. It'll be our last chance to explore this magnificent place. Our time here is up. That is, so long as you're not asking us to prolong our stay?" he inquired in a vaguely combative tone.

Evangelisti lifted his hands again with the backs facing outward, his elbows on the desk, and his eyes looking skyward, a gesture that made him look like a bishop.

"Certainly not! Leave your cell phone numbers with us, so that we can call you if necessary. It's just that . . ."

"Yes?" asked Simona.

"I regret that you won't be staying longer. I would have enjoyed discussing developments in the case with you—informally, you understand," he clarified, with a little smile that gave his unusual face a somewhat disquieting appearance. "I would have liked to have the opinion of two great members of the national police force. And I'm sure that Calabonda would have been happy to have the benefit of your insights."

"I don't know," Simona responded, under Marco's scorching gaze. "We could always change our plans . . ."

*   *   *

The next morning, in a café far from the town center of San Giorgio al Monte, Simona gave a melancholy sigh as she thought back on the lunch at the mountain village osteria. It had been recommended to them by a National Antimafia Commission colleague from Turin, and from the moment they arrived Marco had been imagining it as the apotheosis of his discovery of Piedmontese cuisine. Neapolitan and proud, he regarded the food of the Bay of Naples far above anything existing elsewhere on the planet. Nevertheless, he was curious about "exotic" cuisines, which for him began just beyond Caserta, about twenty miles north of his home city. Yet neither the rosemary aroma of the lard in Cavour; nor the explosion of earthy fragrances in a seed and truffle salad; nor the rich, smooth succulence of the braised meat marinated in Barolo wine for eight days; nor the cheerful scent of violets wafting off the *plaisentif* cheese and mingling with the bouquet of that same delicate flower in a bottle of Barolo Fossati 2000; none of these things had succeeded in altering his expression, which remained as rigid as the marble at Pompeii. His conversation had been reduced to a few monosyllabic words until, having finished scraping the last traces of bonèt from his and Simona's plates, he made up his mind to say:

"I'm guessing you'll prolong your stay here to follow the case."

"Well . . ." Simona stammered. "We could maybe stay another two, three days, don't you think? You wanted to see the murals in Usseaux, and go for a walk in Orsiera Rocciavrè Park, and the day after tomorrow there's the herb festival in Perosa Argentina. We'll be able to try this year's wines . . ."

Faced with this miserable attempt at a diversion, Marco was content simply to sneer in response.

"Fine," he said. "I'll leave tomorrow as planned. I'll keep your friend Michele company in the Aeolian Islands until you decide to honor us with your presence. I'm sure I won't be able to take your place as far as he's concerned, but we did put down a deposit for our stay there, in case you'd forgotten . . ."

Simona didn't try to persuade him otherwise; she knew that he was just as pigheaded as she was. This rams-with-their-horns-locked kind of stubbornness guaranteed something in their relationship that was very rare between people who love each other: true equality. It was a privilege that they paid for with episodes like this one.

Back in the hotel after lunch, Marco had taken a long siesta on the terrace. When the Forensics team had given him back their room, he shut himself off to try to find the guitar chords for a new song that he had written called "Goodnight, Sadness," in homage to his favorite French writer, Françoise Sagan.

Simona returned to police headquarters to see Calabonda.

"Do you have something new for me?" the maresciallo asked when she called to schedule another meeting.

"No, but seeing as I plan to prolong my stay here a bit, I'd like to speak with you."

Calabonda let two or three seconds pass before answering.

"I don't quite understand, but if you'd like, you could come right away."

When he saw her arrive in his office ten minutes later, her white hair covered by a red cap, her nose hidden half by a pair of sunglasses and half by a scarf that was a little out of place on such a mild day, Maresciallo Calabonda couldn't help but raise his eyebrows, though he abstained from making any comment.

"Excuse my disguise," she said, shedding the accessories, "but two national television crews and three reporters— a Roman and two Milanese who I know by sight—turned up in the lobby of the hotel. It's happening just as I was afraid it would: the thought that a weapon belonging to a nationally known antimafia commissario could be used in such a despicable crime was enough to bring them here. I left the hotel through the back exit but eventually they'll trap me and ask for my statement. I think that I'll have to stay."

Calabonda shifted in his swivel chair.

"To me," he demurred, "on the contrary, it seems like a good reason to stick to your plan. You would escape unnoticed, and—if you'll excuse my saying so—it would allow us to work undisturbed in our little corner of the world."

Simona decided that now was the time to exploit her psychological gift for not offending touchy carabinieri in their little corners of the world. She opted for a tone of confidence between colleagues.

"You know that the National Antimafia Commission in general and I in particular have come under attack, by the media and others, for investigations we conducted that implicated several higher-ups in the ruling party. Of the journalists who arrived I recognized one in particular: Bruno Ciuffani, who wrote an editorial accusing me of being in league with the secret society of communist judges that supposedly exists in this country, and of using the investigations to gain exposure for myself at the expense of our elected officials. If I leave tomorrow morning, Ciuffani will say that I'm fleeing my responsibilities so that I can go get a tan in the Aeolian Islands, that I don't give a damn about the investigation into a man's death that was caused by my own imprudence, and that it's an insult to the family's grief."

"But Bertolazzi had no family. He was unmarried, an only child, and his parents are deceased."

"You think that's going to stop them! In the end they'll manage to dig up a girlfriend or an ex-girlfriend who they'll get to talk into a camera, in tears . . ."

"A boyfriend, rather," the maresciallo corrected her. "Bertolazzi was gay, and they say he had many lovers."

"Even better. If they can, they'll dig up a relationship he had with a transsexual, who will denounce my indifference and neglect. They'll have hit the jackpot."

Calabonda stroked his mustache, a sign of deep reflection among the majority of carabinieri, according to literature on the subject.

"So what do you propose?"

"If you'll allow, I think I've developed a certain routine when it comes to media relations, in spite of myself. I propose that you make a statement with me at your side— but I'll be a silent presence. I won't say a word. You will announce that I have made myself available to investigators and that I will remain in San Giorgio al Monte as long as necessary, but that I will abstain from stating my views, so as not to interfere with the investigation."

The proposal was met with a nod of solid assent. But Simona added:

"Still, if you'd like to keep me abreast of developments in the investigation, I'll be happy to listen, and to let you in on some of my thoughts. Perhaps you'll admit that I have some experience in these matters?"

The corners of the maresciallo's mouth, on the verge of lifting upward, suddenly dropped back down toward his chin.

"Yes . . . of course," he said. "That goes without saying. But . . ."

Simona sensed that the official urgently needed to be reassured. *For Pete's sake*, she thought, *these men are always so afraid of losing an ounce of power or prestige!* Nevertheless, she hastened to add:

"But I can look you in the eye and solemnly swear that no matter what happens, this is—and will remain— your investigation."

He frowned, which she interpreted as a sign of confusion. She decided to make sure she had all her bases covered.

"If by chance my . . . thoughts end up being of some use, if they help you to solve the case, I will positively refrain from making them known. Right to the end, I will avoid any and all contact with the pack of dogs that just arrived."

Calabonda grabbed a pen and tapped it against his teeth, making a sound that Simona found irritating in the ensuing silence. She could imagine what he was thinking: *It can only be to my advantage . . . In any case, if she steps on my toes . . .* At last, he set the pen down and smiled broadly.

"I'm sure that I will never be compelled to criticize you to the national press for your lack of cooperation," he said, causing the phrase "piece of shit" to instantly flash across Simona's mind. "And so it will be a pleasure, in an informal capacity, as fellow enforcers of the law—"

He was interrupted by the telephone on his desk. He answered it.

"Yes? ...Ah. Fine, I'll see," he said curtly. Then, hanging up, he explained, "The press . . . They're here, a small army of them, out in front of the main entrance to the building."

"All right then," Simona said, standing up. "Shall we go? Are we in agreement?"

Having gotten to his feet, picked up his cap from the desk, and puffed out his chest, the carabiniere said, "Let's go."

Then, circling around the table to make his way to the door, he squeezed her hand.

"Thank you, Signora Commissario. It will be my honor to hear your . . . thoughts."

Simona was sure that he was about to say "advice."

"And it will be my honor to observe your work," she declared, looking him in the eye.

And now, here she was, in a dingy café on the outskirts of San Giorgio al Monte, about to eat a breakfast of cookies made with corn flour, rye, and chestnuts and sprinkled with chocolate. It would certainly taste good, but she was eating it alone. The idea that Marco—Marco who, unlike nearly every other Neapolitan, preferred the mountains to the sea—would be in the Aeolian Islands by late morning, while she, a sea worshipper who felt oppressed at high altitudes, would be staying put, thrust her into a mood that she absolutely despised. From time to time, the owner behind the counter shot her a look with his bulging eyes then let out a clucking sound he made with his tongue. In front of the bar, a ruddy-faced regular drank his third rum without paying the least bit of attention to her, so completely absorbed was he in indulging his senses in the most extreme, drawn-out, and deliberate way possible. They were the only beings keeping her company on that radiant spring morning that illuminated the windowpanes, with the exception of the deer whose head and horns decorated one of the walls. In its glass eyes Simona seemed to perceive the very same melancholy she felt as she thought of Marco, who would be absently strumming his guitar by the pool of Michele's hotel that afternoon, with a view of Stromboli's smoking volcano, and perhaps also of the ample breasts of a fellow lodger who happened to be traveling alone.

The door opened to reveal a little redheaded man whom she recognized immediately. It was the guy who had been watching them for a long time the day before. He had caught her attention; she had a knack for identifying men from the Services, and this guy reeked of it. If political reputations were at stake, these men would, as they had done countless times before, try to derail the investigation and steer it toward conclusions that benefitted the political power they answered to. Unless it was the political powers that be that answered to the Services—one could never know for sure. Seeing her, the man was slightly startled, which led her to the conclusion that he was either not much of a professional or not very bright. He went to sit at a table near hers and ordered a cappuccino, then began shooting sideways glances at her.

With an exasperated sigh, Simona stood up to face him, picked up a chair, and sat down in front of him, crossing her arms.

The man seemed to wither in his seat. Simona waited until the café owner had brought the cappuccino over and walked away, wearing an increasingly perplexed expression.

"Listen closely," she said almost in a whisper. "I don't know who you work for, whether it's the Department of Information Security, the Intelligence and Current Status Service, or whatever-the-fuck, but right now you leave me alone, because if you don't I'll make a nice statement to the press about harassment at the hands of certain splinter Service groups. I don't know if you understand what I'm getting at, but the adjective 'splinter' has proved harmful in recent years."

"But . . . but . . ." the man stuttered.

He had become violently flushed. Simona's conviction seemed to waver for a moment; but then she told herself that he must simply be a first-rate actor. She took it up a notch.

"Don't you have anything else you could be doing right now? No negotiation down at the docks with a Mafia boss from Naples or Palermo? No arrangements to make to see that a transsexual dies in a fire? No phony bomb plot to organize? Provided you're not the real culprit behind Bertolazzi's murder. Is that it? What's your game—you want to invent a new kind of terrorism? Ecoterrorism? Now I think I'm starting to understand . . ."

Simona had been gradually raising her voice and the café owner was now leaning over the counter. His look of perplexity had given way to a look of resolve.

"Everything all right, Signor Felice? This lady isn't bothering you, is she?"

Simona spun around in her chair.

"How dare you . . ." she started to say. But then she met the angry stare of the café owner, who evidently took her for one of the crazy loner women of a certain age whom one sometimes encounters in coffee shops. She finally admitted to herself that she might be off course.

"Do you know this gentleman?" she inquired.

The café owner nodded vigorously.

"Sure, everyone knows Signor Felice. He's the local reporter for *Il Quotidiano delle Valli.*"

Simona turned back around to face the diminutive man with the carrot-colored hair. He gave her a faint, embarrassed smile and handed her a reporter's badge bearing the information that the café owner had just provided, along with a telephone number. She started breathing again, thinking that no secret agent, no matter how devoted to his organization, would ever accept such a miserable false identity as a cover, for such a long time, on the off chance that something would actually happen in these valleys. It was her turn to turn red.

"Forgive me," she mumbled.

As she was about to stand up, the man held up his badge. Words burst out of his mouth, all jumbled and running into each other as though they'd long been awaiting release.

"Commissario, pardon me by chance would you please grant me an interview?"

The commissario shook her head. She stood motionless for a moment, then sat back down.

"That's impossible. I can't make a statement. I've given my word and I intend to keep it."

She paused, sizing up her conversation partner, who stuck his head straight out from between his shoulders, like a child afraid of being slapped.

"You must be well acquainted with goings-on in the area. Know what we're going to do?"

"What?" murmured the incredibly shy redheaded reporter.

"Let's switch roles this one time. I'll interview *you*. In exchange, I'll let you know the minute the investigation arrives at a conclusion, and you'll be first in line for the story. There's just one condition: you can't reveal your sources, and you have to shine the spotlight on Maresciallo Calabonda and give him all of the credit. Agreed?"

Felice took a sip of cappuccino, both in an effort to give himself an air of dignity and to buy himself some time to think. As he did this Simona decided through an impressive feat of forced logic that, after all, she had only promised Calabonda that she would have no contact with the "pack that had just arrived," and that excluded the local media.

"What do you want to know?" asked Felice, setting down his cup.

"You haven't told me whether we have an agreement."

"All right, all right, sure. Even though the idea of shining that asshole Calabonda's shoes doesn't thrill me, I've always done it; it's my job. I just hoped I'd have the opportunity to do something else . . . So then, what can I do for you?"

The reporter's voice had become more self-assured the more he had talked and the more Simona had smiled at him. He had to admit that she really did have a nice smile.

"What can you tell me about the victim, Bertolazzi, the engineer? All that I know is that he no longer had any family and that he was gay."

Felice flung himself back in his chair.

"Well, he was a local guy. His parents were from here; his father, Maurizio Senior, sold agricultural supplies. Maurizio Junior was born here, went to college in Turin, spent a few years in Africa for Sacropiano. Then he came back and bought himself a nice villa in Torre Pellice. He was responsible for marketing his company's products— genetically modified seeds and pesticides. Which is apparently why the beekeepers singled him out as a target. CCD is causing mass destruction in our area—"

"CCD?"

"Colony collapse disorder. That's when bees stop returning to their hives, all of a sudden and at any time of year, except for in winter, when they go into a state of semi-hibernation. Then you can't find their carcasses, not in the hive and not in the surrounding area. Entire colonies disappear overnight. It's a new phenomenon and highly unusual for such social insects. Oddly enough, the abandoned queen always seems to be in good health and often continues depositing eggs, even though there aren't enough workers left to take care of the brood. The few bees that remain in the hive seem to be lacking in appetite and there's a significant drop-off in their honey production."

"I think there's been a lot written about this."

"Last year 70 percent of the beehives in San Giorgio al Monte and the neighboring towns were affected by the phenomenon. Professor Martini, who lives in our village, studies the trend for a laboratory in Turin; I got all this information from him. And the beekeepers are all up to speed on the issue. They're convinced that pesticides are behind it, in particular the imidacloprid and fipronil produced by Sacropiano, and GMOs, too. There's genetically modified corn in the valley. Those seeds are also sold by Sacropiano.

"But I've also done some research online and the studies that are out there contradict each other. When you get down to it, the causes of CCD still haven't been pinpointed. At any rate, whether or not you approve of Minoncelli and his group's methods, the fact is that it's an extremely disconcerting phenomenon. And not just for beekeepers. To be exact, according to a study universally accepted as irrefutable, 84 percent of plant species cultivated in Europe depend on pollinators, 90 percent of which are bees. More than 70 percent of the products of cultivation, meaning almost all fruit, legumes, oil-producing and protein crops, spices, coffee, chocolate—in other words, 35 percent of the tons of food that we eat—depends on pollination, and given that CCD is a worldwide phenomenon . . ."

Felice's speech had become heated, and the red in his hair seemed to spread to his forehead and cheeks. He kept his eyes locked with Simona's and seemed to be very passionate about what he was saying. Before he could get started on biodiversity and the moon's influence on the harvest, Simona stopped him.

"And you think that this is what led to Bertolazzi's death? That they'd kill him because of his association with Sacropiano?"

"I don't know. At any rate, you can say what you like about Minoncelli—that he's a fanatic, that he'll stop at nothing to save those bees—but he's no killer. Nor is anyone else in his group, for that matter."

Simona smiled with one corner of her mouth.

"You really seem to know a lot about the profile of a killer."

"I've attended seminars given by IASC, the International Association for the Study of Crime."

The commissario nodded. She had heard of this organization, which was Italian in spite of its English name and had been founded by a certain Professor Allegri from Rome and two medicolegal criminologists from Sicily. She had her doubts about its legitimacy, but she kept them to herself.

"I'm very interested in Forensic psychology and criminal profiling. I took the criminal profiling basic training course as well as the advanced course. Full immersion: two eight-hour days of classes, at the end of which you receive a diploma, all with the cooperation of the United Independent Policemen's Confederation," he specified. There was something in his eyes that made Simona wonder if he wasn't the hotheaded one. "Yesterday, I took some photos of the crime scene . . ."

"You went into Minoncelli's house?" Simona was dumbfounded.

"After the Forensics team left. Don't worry, there was no risk of altering the crime scene; they had already finished their survey. I took a few photos with a digital camera I have that allows you to reconstruct a scene in 3-D. I'm thinking of using software tested by IASC. It utilizes neural network technologies in order to simulate the action, with the objective elements discovered at the scene of the crime as a departure point: the position of the body, bloodstain pattern analysis, signs of struggle, repositioned objects, and so on."

"But the bloodstain pattern analysis, you . . ."

"I have a friend in Forensics. Every so often he hands me some information. But I'm just doing this for fun—you know, I don't want to interfere with the investigation."

Simona sighed, mentally filing Felice under "Nutty as a Fruitcake." She resumed:

"And what can you tell me about Bertolazzi?"

Before answering her, Felice waited for his second cappuccino to arrive, along with a croissant, dunking the latter in the former as he spoke.

"I'm sure they've told you Bertolazzi was gay and that he had a turbulent personal life. But that only started recently. For the last three months he was in a steady relationship with a young shepherd, an Albanian man who watches over several flocks of sheep in the pastures in the mountains. Up there," he said, brandishing the croissant in the direction of the windowpanes. But while one end of the pastry was pointed toward the mountaintop, the other, dripping with coffee and milk, was pointing toward the edge of the forest a mere stone's throw away. In precisely that spot a man in a camouflage jumpsuit, unseen by them, was lying on a carpet of pine needles and starting to adjust a Scrome J10 10x40 scope with a Mil-Dot reticle mounted on a STANAG 2324 rail.

As the man framed the door of the café in the scope's crosshairs, Felice explained to an astounded Simona that most cheese from the Italian Alps, Fontina included, was produced using milk from flocks tended by immigrants. Then he returned to the subject of Bertolazzi.

"I wouldn't be surprised if Calabonda considered Mehmet—that's the name of our engineer's lover, Mehmet Berisha—anyway, I wouldn't be surprised if he considered him Suspect Number One. Mehmet is extremely jealous and Bertolazzi was famous for being an incorrigible flirt . . . In fact, he liked to play at seducing women as well as men. Mehmet started one of their usual fights right here the day before yesterday. At this time of day this place is deserted, but you should see it at night—it fills up and becomes very lively. There were a lot of people around when Mehmet told Maurizio that he'd kill him if he had betrayed him. I'm sure that our maresciallo is already up to speed on all of this."

Caught up in what he was saying, he had plunged the tip of the croissant back into the cappuccino. When he didn't bite into it, suspending it somewhere between the cup and his mouth, a big, soft, brown piece broke free and splattered across the table, recalling to this author's mind some (immediately repressed) scatological comparisons. Simona encouraged the reporter to finish his breakfast; they had as much time as they needed. He drank, ate, and threw himself body and soul back into the topic at hand.

"You know, I've given this some thought. Minoncelli is a very handsome man, and, contrary to what one might think, there was more than just hatred between him and Bertolazzi. It's true that the beekeeper would go to the engineer's open information sessions, which were an attempt to dispel the perception in the valley of Sacropiano's GMOs and pesticides as dangerous, and systematically wreak havoc. But then several times I saw them having friendly chats right here at Café Gambetta, and also one time as they were leaving a debate at Claudiana, the bookstore in Torre Pellice, during which they'd argued violently. To tell the truth, I was struck by the extent of the beekeepers' knowledge of Sacropiano's products. Their platform is generally more ideological than scientific, but that time they were very well informed. They even knew the results of some classified studies conducted by the company, in which isolated culture samples indicated that the GMOs could lead to the death of 40 percent of all bees."

Felice paused, staring Simona directly in the eye. The head commissario of the National Antimafia Association, who had come up from the capital, whom he'd seen on television so many times, was hanging on his every word. He inhaled deeply. He no longer felt timid.

"You mean . . . that Bertolazzi could have provided Minoncelli with this information?"

Felice drew his hands back and gave the slightest nod of his chin, his eyes directed skyward—a gesture that was difficult to interpret, but may have meant "maybe."

"And for what reason?"

"I don't know. Bertolazzi was a complex person. It's possible that deep down he doubted the justness of his organization's cause, and it's possible that he thought the beekeepers' group, deep down, wasn't entirely in the wrong. But he may not have had the courage to expose the truth and risk losing his position."

"And how could this tie in with his murder, aside from helping to exculpate Minoncelli?"

"Well, there could be another reason why Bertolazzi would have confided in Minoncelli . . . Have you seen Minoncelli?"

Simona shook her head.

"No. Not yet. As far as I know he's still being held at police headquarters."

"He's a good-looking man. Tall, athletic, blond, and tan, with light blue eyes and enough charisma and smooth-talking to make him the undisputed leader of his group."

"You think Bertolazzi may have been interested in him?"

"I am sure he was interested in him. I could see it when I was watching them talking one on one, even from a distance."

"What do you mean, you could see it?"

"The engineer's eyes would sparkle. It was like he was devouring his conversation partner's mouth with his eyes . . ."

All right, Simona thought, *this Felice guy may not be a secret agent, but as far as snoops go, he's first-rate.* She decided to take full advantage of her informer.

"And could there have been something else aside from the engineer's simple attraction to the beekeeper, something the beekeepers might have exploited in order to get information?"

"It's not impossible. I was passing by Minoncelli's house three days ago, just by chance—"

Just by chance my ass, thought the commissario, but she chose not to interrupt this momentum.

"—and I saw Bertolazzi's car parked in front of his house. So I said to myself, *What have we here! If little Mehmet ever suspected that his beloved was having a secret affair with the beekeeper, things could get ugly . . .* That's what I thought at the time. Funny coincidence, don't you think?"

"That's all very well," Simona said, "but this morning Minoncelli set out to occupy Bertolazzi's villa. Does that seem very friendly to you?"

"What makes you think Bertolazzi didn't give him the keys?"

The commissario pulled back a wisp of white hair that had fallen into her eyes, allowing Felice to see that she was frowning.

"Have you been talking to Calabonda about this?"

Felice snorted.

"The maresciallo won't speak with me and has denied me entrance to police headquarters."

"And why's that?"

The reporter shrugged.

"A stupid mistake. All it took was a single letter to land me in deep shit, I might add."

The commissario raised an eyebrow with an inquisitive expression, while Felice assumed a woeful one. "When he arrived here a year ago and took his place as maresciallo, I dedicated an article to him as a way of saying welcome. But unfortunately I spelled his name incorrectly—I called him '*Caca*bonda'—and from that moment on the nickname has stuck. He can't come into the café without someone calling him that, and seeing as he's made two or three major blunders that had the whole valley cracking up, they've also coined the expression 'pull a Cacabonda,' meaning to really fuck something up."

"Two or three major blunders? What were they?"

Felice crossed his arms.

"Oh no, I'm not telling you. I don't want to make my situation any worse. You'll have many chances to hear about them from other people. You know, Caca—excuse me, *Cala*bonda is already looked down on by his superiors and by a good part of the population. They were talking about transferring him. And so for him this case is double or nothing. If he solves it, he can make up for his mistakes and earn himself national renown. If he fails . . ."

Felice brought his hand up to his shoulder in imitation of someone throwing away something completely worthless.

The commissario's eyes landed on her watch, then rose again.

"By the way, I have an appointment with him in fifteen minutes. I don't want to make him wait."

She extended her hand and the little carrot-haired man stood up to shake it.

"Thank you for agreeing to answer my questions," Felice mumbled, then turned a deep shade of red. "Excuse me," he stammered. "Force of habit."

Simona gave him her brightest smile.

"I hope I get the chance to see you again soon and chat with you some more . . ."

"Well hey," the reporter said, "I come here to drink my cappuccino at the same time every day."

"Then I'll see you tomorrow."

As she was making her way to the door, her cell phone rang. It was Marco. He was dying to let her know that he was embarking for Palermo from the mainland and he'd met a female colleague from the police force while he was waiting for the boat. She was going to be spending fifteen days at the very same little hotel in Salina, Michele's. They'd be riding together on the ferry over. Funny coincidence, no? Apparently the weather down there was magnificent. As Simona asked him how old this lady cop was, and if she was fuckable, and he answered that, well, yeah, she was, and they started fighting, she exited the café and stood near the entrance. The man who was lying at the edge of the forest captured her right at the center of his gunsight. He inhaled deeply. He gently fingered the trigger, but he didn't pull it. And he said, "Pow! You're dead."

CHAPTER 3

SHE HAD ALL OF THE HALLMARKS OF SLOVENIAN ANCESTRY: the rounded curves, the sweet temperament, the golden hair, and a long tongue, apt for licking, sucking, drawing in inexhaustibly. But the male hominids will have to bring their disgusting fantasies to an end at this point, because she was also outfitted with two curved antennae made up of twelve hairy segments, and most important, a highly venomous stinger. Her belly was so full of nectar that it was on the verge of exploding, and it was time to return home. As the *Apis carnica* took flight, the orange-yellow ball lodged in her pollen basket was so large that a few grains fell out onto a pistil whose destiny it was to produce a chestnut, which in turn would eventually become a *marron glacé*. Having just discovered the first blossoming chestnut tree of the year, the lone foraging bee headed for the hive. She was able to use the sun to orient herself, in spite of the dense forest foliage made up of oaks, beeches, and chestnut trees (although how this occurs is still unclear to researchers). As she approached the apiary she was met with a wave of Nasonov pheromones. But unlike her fellow workers, the elderly forager—ten days old already!—could find her way directly to the hive without the aid of these emissions. There she would begin a euphoric, figure-eight dance that would indicate, through careful positioning in relation to the sun, the way to the blooming chestnut tree whose inebriating perfumes she was already conveying to her companions by fanning the scent from her loaded abdomen with her wings. She flew slowly because the tree was at a slight distance. Even though the sky was clouded over, the creature's three so-called simple eyes registered the intensity of the light around her, allowing her to point herself in exactly the right direction, while the eyes on either side of her head viewed the world in shades of dark blue, ultraviolet, orange, and aquamarine through their forty thousand lenses.

This is how she saw the silhouette of the man in the jumpsuit and hood as he made his way among the hives in the apiary: orange and green. He carried an ax and walked in long strides toward the hive where the chestnut-foraging bee's queen was tirelessly laying her eggs. The blade swung, bringing everything crashing to the ground at an incredible speed: the neat stack of perfectly formed flying insects, honey, brood, beehive frames. It all exploded in pulsating waves of chaos, smells, alarm signals, and muted buzzing.

* * *

As Simona entered the courtyard of police headquarters, Maresciallo Calabonda was walking in long strides toward the first of two police cars waiting with engines humming and their sirens already lit. When he saw the policewoman, he gave a little smirk.

"Ah, Commissario. I'm sorry, but I have an emergency," he announced without stopping. "We'll see each other later. Call me sometime before noon," he said as he opened the passenger door.

"Does it have to do with our case?" asked Simona.

"I don't know anything about it," he shot back, with a dubious expression. "I'll keep you informed . . ."

Apparently, he didn't mind letting this star policewoman know who was in charge. As he raised his hand in a gesture of good-bye, the commissario signaled to him to roll down the window.

"You should speak with Felice," she suggested.

Under the effect of a general tightening in his face, the carabiniere's black mustache hairs curled up into his nostrils, hermetically sealing them. Calabonda removed his sunglasses to reveal the lightning bolts shooting out of his eyes.

"The reporter? As though I would waste a moment of my time with that redheaded mythomaniac—it's out of the question!"

With this he nodded at the driver and the car departed, tires shrieking, followed closely by the second car as the sirens began to wail. *Thank God Marco left me with the car*, Simona thought as she set off for the hotel to get their blue, German-built two-cylinder car from the garage. Twenty minutes later she was in Pinerolo. While she was looking for parking in the little street in front of the building, built on an ancient French fortress, her car found itself face to face with a more expensive black vehicle driving down the street. Next to the driver she recognized the wiry frame of Evangelisti, the prosecutor. The magistrate opened the door and got out to shake her hand and speak with her through her rolled-down window.

"I'm headed to the site of another crime . . . Sadly, the crime rate in our region is rising. If you like, you could park your car and join us. We could talk during the drive. It seems it may be connected to our case."

Simona didn't make him say it twice. A few minutes later, the black car was advancing as rapidly as the narrow streets in the city's historic center would allow, its police beacon flashing. The prosecutor turned around and nodded in the direction of the newspaper sitting next to her on the backseat.

"You've become a local celebrity."

Simona picked up the *Quotidiano delle Valli*, which had a photo of her plastered across the front page. It had been taken from her Wikipedia page and was so horribly pixilated that even she struggled to recognize herself in that portly, helmet-haired woman. The headline announced that celebrated antimafia commissario Tavianello was "involved in the murder of Bertolazzi, engineer." That wording was ambiguous to say the least, and the photo caption confused things even further by making it known that she had "agreed to enlighten Maresciallo Calabonda with her counsel." *So that's why the maresciallo was acting so put out when he saw me*, Simona thought. The prosecutor's voice tore her away from her reading.

"Maybe they'll even ask you to be the Man in the Iron Mask next year."

"The Man in the Iron Mask?" Simona repeated, raising her eyes to meet the amused look of Evangelisti in the rearview mirror. "I don't see—"

"The city of Pinerolo was part of the Kingdom of France for many years and it was precisely in our city's fortress that Louis XIV would have kept the famous prisoner. Every year, during the first weekend of October, the legend of the Man in the Iron Mask is commemorated through a costumed event called 'The Man in the Iron Mask and the Musketeers.' Many different groups participate, coming from all over the province of Turin."

The prosecutor paused as the driver sped up to pass a big rig so they could get onto the ramp to a provincial road. For a split second it seemed as though the magistrate wanted to say something to the driver, a little bald man, then decided against it. When they'd overtaken the truck and the car had turned off at a breakneck speed, the policewoman resumed the conversation.

"Yes, that's very interesting, but I don't see what it has to do with me."

Evangelisti smiled and shook his head.

"The Man in the Iron Mask comes to life for the entire weekend in the form of a celebrity whose identity is revealed only at the very end of the festivities, in Piazza Fontana. Last year it was a TV comic, what's his name. Right now his name escapes me . . . Long story short, up until now we've only had men, but I don't see why we shouldn't insist on gender equality in this arena as well."

Seeing as Simona maintained a neutral expression, he changed his tone.

"Well, all joking aside, one might say that our case has become more complicated. There's been another death—"

"Another murder? Where?"

"I didn't say another murder . . . It's still not clear. What's certain is that there's a dead body in Minoncelli's apiary, which has apparently been destroyed."

"But where's Minoncelli? Still at headquarters?"

"He spent the night there and he's still there now, though not for much longer. I won't ask the preliminary investigation judge to order precautionary detention. Based on Forensics' analysis and Minoncelli's statement, Bertolazzi was killed while Minoncelli was at Torre Pellice debating with the owners of Claudiana Books."

They slowly made their way up the great embrace of the mountains, which opened their arms behind

Pinerolo. They crossed bridges that went over streams; there were vertical views, luminous mists, far-off mountain ridges, shaded tunnels made of coniferous trees, and unexpected panoramas. Then they walked across the field behind Minoncelli's house and Simona recalled a passage from the novel *We* by Yevgeny Zamyatin:

> *Spring. From beyond the Green Wall, from the wild, invisible plains, the wind carries the yellow, honeyed pollen from I know not which flowers. This sweet pollen causes the lips to dry out—you are constantly licking them with your tongue—and most likely all of the women one meets have sweet lips (and the men too, of course). This disturbs logical thinking somewhat.*

Beyond the fluttering yellowish cloud, out in the field, the overturned beehives and their contents were spread out across the grass. The commissario, who had never given much thought to beekeeping until that day, felt something akin to grief as she gazed out at it. It was a scene similar in every respect to the ruins of a city after an earthquake. There was something else that she found unsettling, something that it took her a few moments to identify. It was the silence. The men on the Forensics team were surveying the scene and taking photos without speaking a word. Calabonda and his men watched them, their arms crossed. But there was no buzzing to be heard, neither in the flowering pergola where the forager bees had busied themselves the day before nor in the hives. Where had they gone?

As she and the prosecutor drew closer, Simona glimpsed what must have been the body, identifiable more for the technicians circling around it and taking photographs than for its actual appearance. At a distance of ten feet it wasn't easy to decipher a human form in that bundle. One arm appeared from under a pile of frames, honey-filled cells, and mounds of dirt, while a purplish arm covered in bruises and unevenly swollen stuck out from the other sleeve of the T-shirt. The legs, half hidden by the wreckage of the hives, were swollen like those of a drowned body that had been in the water for days. And the face . . .

"What's this?" the commissario asked herself out loud.

She had seen a few Mafia corpses disfigured by sawn-off shotguns and AK-47s, but this . . . this looked like a pumpkin smashed in half.

"Half of the head was attacked by the bees and the other half was torn off by a large-caliber bullet," said a voice with a strong Sicilian accent, adding, "I can't say for certain, but I'd bet it was a .500-caliber, a bullet that could shoot through the armored glass in the front doors of a bank. Maybe shot from a Hecate II, an army rifle used by sharpshooters."

Simona turned around to face the speaker and discovered a short, heavyset man whose furrowed eyebrows gave him an air of perpetual rage—an impression that was probably accurate, because he added, "And don't come bustin' my hump asking me for more, 'cause I'm not in the mood. I haven't even finished the autopsy of the other cadaver and already you're starting in with your questions about this one. What gets into you people up in these mountains? Worse than Sicily! You guys eat dead bodies for breakfast, or what?"

When he'd finished, the man set off, taking large steps toward a German-made utility car parked more crooked than straight near the tasting stand.

"Doctor Pasquano!" the prosecutor yelled at him from behind. "What's the connection?"

The interlocutor got in the car and, before slamming the door shut, yelled, "You'll have it on your desk tonight. You'll get two for the price of one. But don't you dare call me before then."

And he peeled out, with the rear wheels spraying grass and dirt.

"Meet Doctor Pasquano," said the prosecutor with a wry smile. "A consummate professional and a frightening character. He must have lost his poker game last night."

"I think I may have met him before."

"It's possible, if you've been involved in investigations in Sicily. He made his entire career working between Agrigento and Porto Empedocle. He asked to be transferred here a year ago, just like that, after a fight with the commissario. If you ask me, it won't be too long before he's back home."

"My respects, Signor Prosecutor."

The maresciallo had approached them, cap in hand, his gaze fixed on the magistrate, deliberately ignoring the commissario.

"Good day, Maresciallo. Have you reached any conclusions about what might have happened here?"

The carabiniere quickly ran his thumb over his mustache as he straightened his sunglasses with his index finger.

"We have to avoid getting too close to the body until Forensics finishes up. But based on a quick survey, it seems that the victim was bent on destroying the hives with an ax, which you can see down there, a few inches from his hand . . ."

A large blade stuck out among the frames piled up near the body.

"And someone shot him up while he was tearing down the apiary? With a military weapon?"

It was the commissario who had asked the question. The carabiniere turned to look her in the face, as though he were just becoming aware of her presence for the first time. He seemed to hesitate before answering.

"We're listening," Evangelisti said. His use of the first person plural did not seem to please the carabiniere, whose mustache hairs had shot up toward his nostrils again.

"Apparently," he murmured.

He paused, cleared his throat, and nodded in the direction of the attaché case he was holding.

"There's something else," he said somewhat reluctantly. "Another sort of statement . . . We found it under a rock, between the apiary and the perimeter of the forest."

He pulled a sheet of paper in a sealed plastic envelope from the briefcase. On it was written a phrase, in large, red letters: THE WORKER BEE REVOLUTION HAS BEGUN.

"Which reminds me, where have the bees gone?" asked the commissario.

It had just occurred to her that this was what had struck her since their arrival: the silence—the complete absence of that buzzing which the day before had radiated from the flowering roof, from the beehives, and from the edges of the forest, permeating the atmosphere around them.

The maresciallo removed his sunglasses to get a better look at her. Something like a smirk, halfway between profound bewilderment and vague disdain, appeared on his lower lip. "I don't know anything about that," he declared. "And to tell the truth, I don't see what it has to do with the investigation."

"You find a sheet of paper referring to the 'Worker Bee Revolution,' the bees have disappeared, and you see no link whatsoever?" Simona insisted.

Stone-faced, the carabiniere abstained from comment. Evangelisti cleared his throat.

"But you've managed to get a hold of Bertolazzi's lover, the Albanian shepherd . . . what was his name?"

"Mehmet Berisha. No, we still haven't found him but we're actively looking. There will be a search in the pastures up in the mountains soon."

The maresciallo's eyes settled on a point beyond where the commissario stood.

"Look," he said, "here's someone who may be able to answer your questions about the bees."

The magistrate and the policewoman turned. A bright-red microcar of the kind so small it can be driven without a license in Italy advanced over the grass, lurching precariously. It stopped, parked, and from the little front compartment emerged a tall bald man with glasses. He unfurled his limbs like a huge, lanky insect and made his way toward the trio with large steps.

"I know who the killer is!" he screamed as he came toward them. "I know who the killerrrr issss!"

As he came closer, Simona could make out his wide-open eyes, his manic appearance. The man stopped six feet from the group, out of breath.

"I know who the killer is!" he repeated a third time.

"Which killer?" the prosecutor inquired in a neutral tone.

"The one who killed the men that died. Bertolazzi. And the dead man here, in the apiary."

"Ah, so you know?" Evangelisti resumed.

"Yes, sorry; your little mystery novel is over. You may have been hoping to keep us guessing with this story, but it's all over. No more suspense. I'll reveal the guilty party's name. The end."

He crossed his arms, his body planted squarely on his legs, and eyed them one after the other: first the maresciallo, then the magistrate, then Simona.

"So?" said this last one.

The man sighed and lowered his eyes as though caught off guard.

"To be more exact," he said in a voice that had abruptly become hesitant, "I can tell you who gave the order. It doesn't matter who carried it out."

"That's your opinion. But the orders, they came from . . ."

"The bees."

Silence.

"The bees?" repeated Simona.

The man nodded.

"The bees."

The magistrate sighed.

"Commissario Tavianello, allow me to introduce Professor Aldo Martini, a native of these parts and a nationally known bee researcher. His observations have been very useful to beekeepers in the region."

"Too bad he has those raving fits," the maresciallo chortled. "You'll have to excuse me, Signor Prosecutor, Signora Commissario, but some routine duties await me."

And after a quick military salute, he turned on his heel.

"Professor Martini," Evangelisti said, "I have no doubt that your reasoning, your attributing the ultimate responsibility for these murders to the bees, is worthy of attention . . . I know that in addition to being a great scientist you are also an exceptional speaker. I attended one of your lectures. You have a way of taking brilliant paradoxes and masterfully weaving them together. But you see, like Caca—Calabonda, I also have a few routine duties to attend to. You wouldn't want to get too close to the crime scene, right, Professor? So as not to disturb the investigators' work . . ."

Martini shrugged.

"Certainly," he said. "God forbid I should take up their valuable time. Their time is their own; let them do with it as they wish."

The magistrate sighed, then turned to Simona.

"As for us, we'll get back to the city. I don't believe there's anything happening here for us to stick our noses into, for the time being."

"If you don't mind," the commissario said, "I'll stay a little longer. I'd like to chat with the professor a bit. I'll take a cab back."

The confused prosecutor raised an eyebrow as if he wanted to say something and shot a look in Martini's direction. But all he said was, "As you wish. I'll see you later. Good-bye, Professor."

When they were alone Simona asked, "First of all, can you explain to me where the bees went?"

A look of profound stupefaction appeared on Martini's face.

"But . . ." he said. "Then you've really understood?"

CHAPTER 4

*U*P ABOVE THE HARSH LANDSCAPE OF LOCRI, Calabria, or Sicily's lush Madonie mountains, over the course of various police operations—hunts for fugitives, raids on Mafia clans, missions to free captives—Simona had had many opportunities to survey the mountains from a helicopter. The fact that the horizon line would pitch unexpectedly, that you grazed the treetops, that you could drop like a stone or shoot back up vertically, separated from the oblivion below by nothing but a sheet of glass that suddenly seemed too thin—none of this fazed Simona in the least. With a glance behind her, she confirmed that the other passengers were less accustomed to all this. The pallor of Calabonda's face made his mustache and sunglasses seem even blacker than usual, whereas Evangelisti was dripping sweat in spite of the blasts of cold wind coming in from the openings on either side of them. Even though she wasn't afraid, Simona noticed that the pilot didn't seem terribly concerned about his passengers' well-being. As they drew near the summit of Mount Banchetta the chopper tilted upward at a forty-five-degree angle, first on one side, then the other, executing a series of excruciating turns in order to keep to the outer edges of the larch trees. The cows below them sometimes came so close that it seemed they could look them in the eyes.

She eyed the pilot, a burly young man in jeans and a short-sleeved button-up shirt. He had the intent expression of a serious professional on a difficult mission. But something worried her. The large, padded headset hooked up to the radio system was resting on the pilot's shoulders, and he had a couple of white tablets stuck in his ears with a thin cord connecting them to his shirt pocket . . . He wasn't tuned in to the radio control tower; he was listening to his iPod. Without even thinking about it, the commissario reached out a hand and brought one of the earphones close to her own ear.

"Da-na-na, na! DA-NA-NA-NA, NA! DA-NA-NA-NA, NA!"

The crescendo made her immediately reinsert the earphone in the man's ear. He turned toward her and gave her a big smile.

"The Ride of the Valkyries," he yelled over the roar of the engine. "Have you seen *Apocalypse Now*?"

She nodded.

"I love the smell . . ." she started to say in English, practically shouting.

". . . of napalm in the morning," he finished, absolutely ecstatic. "Wow! Now that's cinema!" he yelled as he yanked the cyclic control and the top of a fir appeared suddenly in their field of vision, only to disappear a half-second later.

"Goddamn it, be careful!" Calabonda burst out.

The pilot's only reply was to give a thumbs up, like a Yankee about to gun down a Vietnamese village.

Simona passed a hand through a wisp of her white hair. *Another lunatic*, she thought. *Maybe it's the mountain air.* First there was Felice, the "red-headed mythomaniac," as the maresciallo had called him, whom, at any rate, she was sure to see the following day. Not so much because she was curious to know the results of his technology based neural-network program's analysis, but because she wanted to draw out some more details about the local situation. After the reporter, it would be bee specialist Professor Aldo Martini's turn.

* * *

"But, then you've really understood?" he had asked when she had questioned him on the bees' disappearance from the devastated apiary.

"Understood what?" she had shot back. He responded with a bewildered gaze.

"I'm sorry, I was mistaken. Even with everything that's happened, they're still all just theories . . ."

"What are you talking about? I don't understand. And, first of all, why do you say that the bees are sending the killers?"

He gave her a wide smile that was friendly and disarming.

"Did I really say that?"

"Yes, Professor, you said it yourself, to Maresciallo Calabonda, Prosecutor Evangelisti, and me."

"Ah, I'm sorry. You know, I do have raving fits sometimes. I'm schizophrenic. Calabonda knows. That's why he doesn't let me get to him."

He kept smiling, and seemed to be wondering what she was doing there.

"How can I be of service?" he said after a few moments of silence.

"If you have a minute, perhaps we could find a quiet spot," she proposed, with a wave of her hand to indicate the carabinieri and Forensics workers walking around Minoncelli's destroyed hive. "So that you can tell me a bit about the bees. And about the cause of their disappearance."

At the wheels of their respective cars, they made their way to the town center of San Giorgio al Monte and ended up in a tea salon, where he took it upon himself to order two pieces of gianduja torte and two cups of Darjeeling before explaining his theory that the bees were dying because they had overadapted. Loaded with the pesticides and organophosphates they gathered, even up on the summits of the Alps, their bodies had undergone a mutation at the immune level. Simona's cell phone rang as the professor launched into various scientific explanations. It was Marco. She didn't answer, but it was distraction enough to make it impossible for her to pick up where she left off in his line of reasoning. She only remembered that, according to Martini—and he himself had used this metaphor—the bees were dying as a result of an attempt to adapt too well to changes in the world around them, rather than resisting them. "Exactly like a certain faction of the left in this country," the professor concluded.

* * *

"We're here," Calabonda shouted from behind Simona.

Overtaking a fortified crest formed by the tops of larch trees, the helicopter reached a valley in which acres and acres of pastureland sprawled toward a great wall of slate-colored mountains, spotted with snow that was dazzlingly bright. Simona's face was struck full on by the visual slap of the undulating pinks, violets, whites, and golden yellows of the asters, buttercups, snowbells, flowering moss, and violets of Moncenisio that covered the fields. *Almost as beautiful as the sea*, she admitted mentally.

"It's over there," Calabonda announced, pointing to a little grassy hill where one could make out, near a penned-in area where a flock of several hundred sheep were gathered, a little one-story construction.

Right next to an enormous, curved rock, there was an unadorned structure made of flat, unmortared stones. The same stones comprised the single-pitched roof, which sloped down to the door, and two windows that seemed to be the only openings. At the foot of the little hill three sports utility vehicles belonging to the State Forestry Corps were parked at the end of a dirt road. A dozen men wearing camouflage jumpsuits and armed with sniper rifles could be seen positioned in a semicircle around the building at a distance of one hundred feet.

"Excellent," said the maresciallo, with the pair of binoculars he kept hanging around his neck glued to his eyes. "The deployment looks airtight to me."

Simona locked eyes with Evangelisti, whose face seemed to express much less confidence than the carabiniere's voice. The prosecutor's phone call had caught her as she was exiting the tea salon, where she had left Professor Martini to finish devouring the second piece of gianduja torte. The magistrate had suggested they meet as soon as possible at the heliport behind headquarters; they had found Mehmet Berisha, the Albanian shepherd. He had fired a shot as the carabinieri were closing in and now they were waiting for reinforcements so they could arrest him. If she wished, she could be present for the arrest and for the first interrogation. Now the aircraft was touching down in a great cinematic whirlwind of bending grasses, soldiers stooped over with their hands covering their headgear, and crackling radios. As the blades made their last revolutions, turning more and more slowly, the passengers left the field and, surrounded by carabinieri in bulletproof vests and helmets, arrived at the road. Behind an escarpment that shielded the sheep from view, near the parked cars, a paunchy brigadier greeted them with a military salute.

"The deployment is in action," he declared. "The subject can only exit through the front; there are no side openings, and only stone in back. The shooters are aimed at the windows and the door," he explained, gesturing toward a bed of rhododendrons in bloom higher up in the sloping meadow, about a hundred feet from the sheepfold.

Simona screwed up her eyes and made out three carabinieri lying down in the grass at the base of the shrubs with their submachine guns pointed at the little building. A little farther off on the right, behind a watering trough, she saw another three soldiers crouched down with their left hands resting on their grenade launchers. There were more men, carabinieri or forest rangers, lying on the grass to the left and right. The brigadier held out a megaphone and a gas mask to the maresciallo.

"Whenever you want to give the signal . . . we're ready to strike," he concluded with a twitch of his legs that made it apparent he had restrained himself from fully clicking his heels. Calabonda took the objects that had been handed to him.

"All right," he said, turning toward the prosecutor. "If you're ready, let's go."

"One second," Evangelisti cut in. "First give me a detailed account of what happened," he said, speaking to the brigadier.

The latter shot a look in the direction of the maresciallo, who nudged his sunglasses up his nose with his index finger and with a nod of the chin prompted his subordinate to answer.

"Following your instructions, Maresciallo, I left headquarters at ten o'clock with two men, in the jeep belonging to Alio from the Forestry Corps, who drove. We parked here and then we climbed up the escarpment and began walking toward the area where the sheep are kept. And all of a sudden, a shot from a firearm. We dropped to the ground. I yelled, 'Carabinieri! Come out with your hands in the air.' Several seconds went by, then the subject yelled something in his language from inside. He seemed very agitated."

"What did he yell?" Simona asked.

The brigadier turned around to face her and looked her up and down. He apparently recognized the famous policewoman whose photo had been published in the *Quotidiano delle Valli*, because he smiled and responded right away, this time without asking for permission from his superior. "I don't know, Commissario. I don't speak Albanian."

"Could you try to reproduce the sounds?" Simona insisted. "I've learned some of the language investigating the Albanian Mafia," she explained, facing the prosecutor.

The brigadier scratched his head.

"I wouldn't know. Something like 'brakala.' He repeated it many times."

The policewoman frowned. She didn't respond.

"Another question," she said, returning to action. "You say there was another detonation. But are you sure it came from the sheepfold?"

The carabiniere seemed disconcerted and let two or three seconds pass before answering. "One hundred percent sure? It's hard to say. The detonation echoed across the mountains . . . but I can't imagine who else . . ."

"Listen," the maresciallo said with an irritated cluck of the tongue. "It seems clear enough to me. Right? If he wasn't the one to fire the shot, why would he refuse to leave the sheepfold?"

"That's true," noted Evangelisti.

"All right. Let's go," the maresciallo said. "Proceed as directed."

Calabonda removed the walkie-talkie from his belt and raised it to his mouth.

"Permission to command the sharpshooters. Granted?"

"Granted!" shouted the machine.

"I'll be right there," the maresciallo said. "Cover me."

The exchange seemed to reverberate throughout the entire valley. *If the other guy didn't hear it,* Simona thought, *he must be deaf.* And then she found herself running, hunched forward, alongside the maresciallo. When they had made it to the foot of the purplish rhododendron bushes and the maresciallo realized he had been followed by the commissario and the prosecutor, he let out an exasperated sigh but said nothing. Lying down on the grass, he took a minute to catch his breath, then asked the snipers, "Are all of the openings in check?"

The three men responded one after the other.

"Right window in check."

"Door in check."

"Left window in check."

Calabonda flashed his teeth in a smile.

"So I guess you don't think that training I put you through was so pointless after all!" he mumbled, then brought the walkie-talkie up to his mouth. "Tear gas squad, are you ready to fire on my signal?"

The volume of the other walkie-talkies was set so high that the maresciallo's question bounced back to them from the watering trough, reverberated by the surrounding peaks. Simona shook her head, but she kept quiet.

"We're ready," barked Calabonda's walkie-talkie.

He set the gas mask on the ground, then grasped the handle of the megaphone in one hand, taking the microphone, connected to the speaker by a spiral cord, in the other.

"Mehmet Berisha," he began, but there was such a loud squeal of feedback that everyone present brought their hands up to their ears. The maresciallo adjusted a knob and continued.

"Mehmet Berisha . . ."

Someone screamed from inside the sheepfold. Simona stared at the structure, trying to interpret those sounds, thinking they vaguely resembled something. "Brakala"? No, that wasn't it. "Brokala"? "Brokkanlé"? What was the shepherd saying?

"This is Maresciallo Calabonda speaking. Come out immediately with your hands in the air or we will be compelled to use force."

The voice screamed again, and then again. Then silence returned to the valley.

The maresciallo let several seconds pass, shrugged, and ordered into his walkie-talkie, "A grenade in each opening."

There were three almost simultaneous detonations. At the end of their smoking parabolas, one of the grenades fell six feet from the door, and another ricocheted against the stone wall and rolled not far from the first. They began to diffuse a dense white smoke that the wind spread toward the watering trough, where the men began to cough, and toward the sheepfold, where the sheep bleated and made a mad dash for the other end of the enclosure. The third grenade went through the window.

Inside, the man continued to shout the same sounds, except that his voice had become shrill.

"Fuck," said Simona, finally understanding. She jumped to her feet and without stopping grabbed a gas mask as she set off for the building.

"What are you doing?" shouted Calabonda. "Come back immediately. Don't shoot!" he screamed into the megaphone at full volume.

As the maresciallo's command thundered across the meadow, causing several marmots to make a run for it and a couple of pheasants take flight, to the disappointment of the fox that had been watching them, salivating, another "Come back!" resounded to a distance of two miles. A startled wolf on the rocky mountain terrain crossed one paw over the other, setting off a mini-landslide, chasing away some wild goats. The sound of a third call accompanied by an expletive rose up through a granite gully until it reached a bald eagle, which turned its round, astonished eyes on the tiny creatures below. Simona realized with a touch of pride that she had not run out of breath yet.

But by the time she reached the smoke-filled entrance to the sheepfold she had lost it. The situation did not improve when she had to put on the mask. She struggled to attach it, coughed, fought the urge to spit, and raced inside.

Two minutes later, when she emerged dragging the inanimate, incredibly heavy body of the stocky little shepherd, she had no more breath, no more strength, no more anything.

She tore off the mask and surrounded by milky-white, poisonous spirals that immediately made her eyes tear up, she yelled at the figures rushing toward her, surrounding her, and pointing their weapons at the man lying on the ground: "*Broken leg! Broken leg!*"

She couldn't stop her lungs from inflating, desperately seeking oxygen. She swallowed a big mouthful of gas and muttered, "It's English, you assholes."

And she threw up.

"English," she repeated. "Not Albanian."

And she threw up again.

They helped her to her feet and walked her against the wind, away from the smoke. She spat abundantly, cleared her throat, and turning toward the carabinieri crouched at the shepherd's side, screamed in a voice that was clearly used to giving orders, "Emergency medical evacuation!"

Then she freed herself from the brigadier's hand, which had continued to hold her up by one arm. "This man is gravely wounded," she said to him. "He had a broken leg, shattered by a bullet. They shot him."

"What do you mean, they shot him? But it was him . . ."

She shook her head.

"The shot was not fired from the sheepfold. Search it. I would be amazed if you found a gun—at any rate, a gun that had been used recently."

Evangelisti drew near, out of breath.

"You really gave us a fright. Is the wound serious?"

"Given the extent of the damage," she said to him, "I wouldn't be surprised if the bullet were of the same caliber as the one that killed the man in the apiary. He's lost a lot of blood. I hope he makes it. If not, someone will need to explain why enforcers of the law attempted to asphyxiate him rather than come to his aid."

The maresciallo, after speaking with the group that was transporting the shepherd on a stretcher, walked toward them, as the prosecutor whispered in Simona's ear, "There, now you understand the meaning of the expression 'to pull a Cacabonda.'"

Of course, that was the moment that Marco chose to call her back, demanding to know why she had been unreachable for the entire morning.

* * *

Since the helicopter was being used to transport the wounded man, they all crammed into the State Forestry Corps's SUVs. Simona avoided climbing into the same vehicle as Calabonda. After some hesitation, Evangelisti decided to go with the maresciallo. The commissario found herself sitting next to an attractive female corps member, whose uniform, with each of the innumerable jolts caused by the rough terrain, almost failed to contain her generous, ricocheting bosom. Her name was Anna and she had a passion for emerging technologies. She explained to Simona the potential significance, in her opinion, of a pilot project still in the early stages. The project consisted of capturing the greatest possible number of animals in Val Troncea National Park in order to implant radio frequency identification chips under their skin before freeing them. This would allow them to track their movements for the rest of their lives.

"Do you realize what this means? At any given moment, we'll know the location of every animal in the park. We'll be able to protect the flocks of sheep without having to shoot down a single wolf, and control overly populous animals by eliminating them with precision."

"But do you think this technique could be applied to humans as well?" Simona asked.

"Could it?" said the Forestry Corps member excitedly. "You've hit the nail on the head. You've grasped the real significance of the project! The question isn't *if* but *when*. The chip is the final step in a process that began the day someone had the idea to assign a number, the fiscal code, to every Italian citizen at birth. This number already contains the data of one's name, date and place of birth, etcetera. In the past this number has been printed on an identification card and then stored on a microchip along with other information. All of this is ultimately leading up to the simpler option: putting the chip under people's skin. In my opinion, in twenty, thirty years from now, every one of us will have a subcutaneous implant, which will function both as a document of identification and a credit card. And you know what else? These chips will interact with chips in the products we put in our shopping carts and with those in the supermarkets' cash registers. All we'll have to do is walk near the registers and everything we've bought will be added up and deducted directly from our bank accounts. The same for transportation, the same everywhere—which will ultimately mean the disappearance of physical currency. These chips will allow us to enter buildings we are authorized to enter, eliminating the need to present our documents. The chips in all human beings and all objects will 'talk' to one another; there will be supplies of products that, from thousands of miles away, will announce to other supplies that they are about to run out, reminding people to replenish them. Then those people will feel an electric impulse telling them to consult a screen and the products will be sent where they're needed . . . Do you understand what that means?"

"Yes, I think I do. You are surprisingly well informed."

The young woman shot her a sarcastic look.

"You think that forestry rangers are just a bunch of rubes?"

Simona shook her head. Anna went on.

"I belong to a group of technophiles here in the valley. We're part of a global network of people who discuss the future applications of science. We are 100 percent in favor of the theory of the 'superhuman.'"

"What would that be?"

Anna opened her mouth to answer but the SUV stopped abruptly. Several roe deer appeared in the shade of the trunks of the larch trees that ran along the side of the road. One of them turned its delicate muzzle toward the vehicle and its black eyes seemed to survey the extent of the damage in that hominid-filled mass of metals. The passengers sat in silence while the engine hummed pleasantly. In a few graceful leaps, four animals crossed the road, their hooves just barely touching the ground.

"We're entering into a new cycle of technological development that will transform mankind," the forest ranger began again. "By that I mean NBCC, which stands for nano-, bio-, computer, and cognitive technology. These sciences will converge to modify the very nature of man, accelerating his development, so that he ceases to be *Homo sapiens* and becomes superhuman. You'll find it difficult to believe if you don't know the facts, but we could eventually succeed in conquering aging and death."

"Yes, it's true: I'm not up on the facts, and I do find it difficult to believe," Simona admitted. As they emerged from a bend in the road, she looked out at the alpine village of Sestriere, with its motionless towers and its large, motionless buildings, the stretches of barren terrain used as ski slopes and the weather vanes that greeted the Italian national soccer team on a pre–World Cup retreat.

She coughed, determined to show interest.

"To return to the subject of the subcutaneous chip, tell me, do you think it could be of some help to us, as enforcers of the law?"

"Of course. Imagine the possibilities it could open up. We'll be able to track anyone at any given moment; people will be incapable of getting lost, incapable of disappearing.

Children, or Alzheimer's sufferers, or people under house arrest who moved too far beyond the confines of their homes would set off an alarm. But there's more. Let's imagine where it could go from there in just a short time. The moment a crime is detected, video surveillance cameras—they're widespread now, but one day they'll be everywhere—these video cameras will not only sound the alarm, they'll instantly register the coordinates of the criminal, recording his every movement. Of course, any attempt to remove the chip from under the skin would set off an alarm."

"But aren't these kinds of projects met with opposition?"

"Oh, the usual enemies of progress. And the self-proclaimed defenders of human rights. As if humanity's first right, the most important right of all, weren't the right to safety . . . Don't you agree?"

When Simona didn't respond, she insisted:

"At any rate, if we haven't done anything wrong, it shouldn't bother us that we're being watched, right?"

When the commissario still refused to speak, the pretty forest officer burst out, "Do you have any idea how significant our park's experiment will be, if this project gets approval? Thanks to research conducted here, in the not-so-distant future every one of us will be traceable at any given moment, with a real-time chronology of all our movements, all our purchases, all our actions! It's brilliant, don't you think?"

"Yes, brilliant . . ." Simona said, thinking she had yet another piece of evidence to support her theory about the mountain air.

*   *   *

Two hours later, when she was speaking with the Gnone brothers of the Claudiana bookstore in Torre Pellice, she had to admit it might be wrong to extend her psychiatric analysis to all of the valley's inhabitants. Clearly, these two weren't the least bit crazy. They confirmed that they'd exchanged a few words with Minoncelli around eight, before they'd even opened the store. Which meant that he could not have killed Bertolazzi.

"We were standing right here," Massimo said, gesturing to indicate the little room set up at the center of the store, with shelves of books on either side.

"Minoncelli was talking about organizing a debate for members of a group of technophiles in the valley."

"Oh right," Simona said. "I was just talking to someone about that stuff."

"That stuff," Stefano intervened, "as you call it, is the antenna of a network of people in our valley in favor of emerging technologies, funded by all the big biotechnology companies, Sacropiano among them. Now, according to Minoncelli, who has at least one informant in Sacropiano—"

"Has, or had?" interrupted Simona.

The two brothers exchanged a glance. Then Massimo said slowly, "I see you're caught up on the facts."

"Was Bertolazzi his informant?"

Stefano shrugged.

"Since you seem to be caught up . . . Minoncelli told us in confidence that he'd gotten his information directly from the engineer. According to him, the company was planning to branch out into nanotechnology with an experiment that consisted of attaching microchips to every bee in an apiary, in order to better understand colony collapse disorder."

"The syndrome that causes domestic bee colonies to dissolve," Massimo clarified. Simona nodded.

"I'm familiar with it."

"According to Minoncelli, Sacropiano intended to use the technophiles in the valley to gain support for the idea. And he wanted to organize a public debate to oppose it."

"But what's Minoncelli fighting for? To protect his apiaries, or does he have a broader objective? What I mean is, could he belong to a party, an organization, outside of his circle of activists?"

"Not that I know of," Massimo said. "He opposes the artificialization and commoditization of living beings."

"To be totally honest, we're on his side, even if we don't always approve of his methods," Stefano added.

Massimo stood up and walked over to the coffee machine behind the desk next to the store's entrance.

"Coffee?" he offered.

"Gladly."

There was a pause, which Simona took advantage of to mull things over. A short while before, as they were turning off of the highway and onto the driveway to headquarters, the prosecutor had let her know that he'd received several phone calls during the drive down the dirt road.

"First of all," he had announced, "Berisha is out of the woods. The doctors are keeping him in isolation for the time being, but they say we'll be able to question him tomorrow. Secondly, the man who destroyed Minoncelli's apiary before being shot down by a large-caliber bullet has been identified: a certain Danela, also a beekeeper. Calabonda will have his men gather as much information on him as possible. I'll have that report this evening, along with Pasquano's report on the autopsies of Bertolazzi and Danela. Then we'll be able to take stock of the situation. The last piece of news is that there are television crews stationed outside of the Pinerolo court building and in front of your hotel. There's no doubt that they're waiting for you. What would you like to do, come to the court building with me? I can give you an office to use. Or if you'd rather go back to your hotel, I can ask the maresciallo to send you two or three men to keep the pack at bay."

"I think I'll go do a bit of sightseeing around Torre Pellice instead," she had answered. And now, here she was, on the verge of tasting the Gnone brothers' excellent coffee, trying to draw a connection between the initiatives of a multinational corporation, the theft of her gun with the intent of killing an engineer, the destruction of Minoncelli's apiaries, colony collapse disorder . . .

"But is it for real, this business about microchips being affixed to bees?" she asked after a somewhat over-sweetened sip.

Stefano set his cup down and shifted his body in the large armchair where so many excellent authors on book tours had placed their behinds.

"Technically, I think it's feasible, with nanotechnology. If you'd like," he added, pointing toward the back of the store, "we have everything you need to read up on the subject right here."

"Do the two of you think there could be some relationship . . . ?"

Massimo smiled. "You're the police officer, aren't you?"

Stefano looked at his watch, and Simona hastened to say, "Just one or two more questions, then you'll be able to reopen the store. What do you think of Felice, the reporter? Is he trustworthy, in your opinion?"

"Oh," said Massimo, "he's like any member of the technophiles . . ."

Ah, so he's part of this thing too, thought Simona. *No surprise there.*

"A bit of a hothead . . ." Stefano added. "But he's very serious about what he does. He tries to do his best work, which doesn't always correspond to the needs of Dottore Signorelli, the head of the *Quotidiano delle Valli*."

"And what do you think of Professor Martini?"

Massimo laughed. "I see that in two days you've managed to meet all of the valley's true characters. If you're basing your judgment on them, you must have a strange opinion of the locals."

"Not at all," Simona lied.

"Martini is a little like Felice. Apart from the fact that he is clearly more disturbed. But he seems to be a prominent specialist in his field. He's been called into many towns as a consultant."

"Good," said Simona.

She thought for a few seconds. Then: "One last question. What is there to see in Torre Pellice?"

CHAPTER 5

*A*T NINE O'CLOCK ON THAT JUNE night it was still broad daylight on the rock-strewn western face of the mountain. Enormous, oblong rocks pierced the terrain on a diagonal like porpoises, dolphins, and whales leaping through a sea of stones. In front of one of these masses, at the edge of a little stream trickling down from the snow around the eastern limits of the alpine precipice, the man set down his backpack and his weapon. Lying on the cold stone with his face directed toward the rays of an invisible sun, he listened closely, hearing only the sound of his own breath, which was heavy from the climb. Then his breathing became calm, fading into the total silence of the peaks. He stayed that way for several long minutes, completely still, with his equipment between his splayed legs and his heels planted among the stones. After some time had passed, he heard a loud, faraway crack: the colliding horns of mountain goats competing for females. It continued for a little while then ended abruptly. Silence again.

Until a whistle came from the direction of the lake and the far reaches of the meadows below. Several marmots scattered in fear.

After that, the faintest sound of hoof beats, of rolling stones, the swish of flying. Maybe a snow partridge disturbed by a weasel, a dormouse, or a field mouse.

Then nothing again, for a long time.

Finally, he heard it. The sound he had been waiting for. A buzzing like nothing else. And he saw it, a flying pearl of light in the sunset. It advanced toward him. Then, about three feet from his face, its four wings whipping the air at two hundred forty beats per second, it veered off again in the other direction, making a large figure eight. The man observed the bee's dance at length—its orientation with respect to the sun, its very slow movements. He smiled, picked up his weapon, and started walking. And as he waded across a rushing stream, stood on an overhang, walked over the patches of melting snow, the bee took off again in the direction from which it came, continually reappearing and departing again. One could say that it was showing him the way.

*　*　*

In her mind, Simona went over the menu of the meal she had just eaten for the sixth time. She had been treated to dinner at the Crota dl'Ours by the director of the library at the Waldensian cultural center. At the end of the meal, Walter Eynard, the chef, had insisted that she taste several varieties of mountain grappa, and the commissario was afraid her mind was sinking into oblivion.

Now, having just crossed the threshold of the hotel lobby, she cherished the thought of a long phone conversation with Marco. But no sooner had she set one foot on a rug on which several deer were shown fleeing some hunters than she heard her name being called by a very familiar voice.

"Commissario Tavianello!"

From behind the backrest of a sofa facing away from the entrance and tucked in a corner of the lobby appeared a face with hollow cheeks and a bluish beard beneath a crown of tousled hair. The man, who must have been completely lying down, performed a strange gymnastic routine in order to get upright and scale the backrest, which he did with an athletic leap. Bruno Ciuffani, television news presenter, made sure it was known by everyone, especially the audience of his show *La Mosca*, that he was an athlete, ran in the New York marathon, rooted for Lazio's soccer team, etcetera—all things that had become indispensable to the arsenal of a populist media personality, a personality that had come to be valued very highly by the station's managers in recent years. Simona made a beeline for the elevator but Ciuffani caught her in front of the control panel.

"Leave me alone," the policewoman said. "I'm tired."

In that same instant a man with a camera on his shoulder appeared from behind a pillar and a microphone materialized under Simona's nose.

"Does the fact that you allowed a murderer to steal your weapon make you especially qualified to lead this investigation?" the reporter attacked, as a chiming sound heralded the elevator's arrival. "Wouldn't it be better to attempt an act of modesty for once and leave these legally trained and qualified investigators alone to do their jobs?"

The light on the camera forced Simona's eyes shut, but she did her best to keep them open and maintain a stony expression. She didn't feel like taking another low blow along the lines of "the commissario's only reply to our valid questions was a mocking and disdainful sneer." The doors opened and she vaulted inside without saying a word or trying to block them from entering, knowing from experience that any attempt to ward off an intrusive camera would look on-screen like a reprehensible attack on the freedom of the press and the right to information.

"Is it true that you blocked a police operation with the sole intent of protecting an Albanian man, a non–European Union national and a suspect in the murders of Bertolazzi the engineer and Danela the beekeeper?"

The elevator stopped. The camera's lens drew even closer to the commissario's face and the question came out before the elevator doors could open:

"Is it true that you argued with your husband, Police Chief Tavianello, because he disapproved of your intent to meddle in this investigation?"

Simona felt her stomach drop and couldn't keep a wince from spoiling her pretty face. The doors opened.

She turned her back on the television crew and motioned to leave, but before touching down on the hall floor, her right foot flew back and slammed into the cameraman's shin. She turned around to say "Excuse me" as she brought her heel down on the marathon runner reporter's big toe, leaning as far back as she could and grinding her foot into him as though she were stomping something into the ground.

"I shouldn't have," she admitted a few minutes later, when she was finally stretched out on the bed. "But I couldn't help myself."

* * *

"You say you shouldn't have done it, but it was good for you," Marco pointed out. "So you did the right thing. After all, we can't let them step on our toes all the time without ever fighting back. What are you doing?"

"Nothing. I'm giving my foot a deep massage with one hand. It helps."

"That must be why you're breathing a little heavily. It's . . . almost provocative." Simona let go of the sole of her left foot, to which she had been applying a series of thera- peutic squeezes, and settled into a comfortable position on the pillows in order to speak more evenly.

"You know, it's strange what's happening to me in this little corner of the mountains," Simona said. "I know you think I'm wasting my time. And yet I have this feeling that something very significant is going on here, something bigger than the two murders."

Marco grumbled.

"So you didn't stay just because you were ticked off about having your gun stolen to kill somebody? You're genuinely interested in this case? You think it has some implication or other?"

"Yes, implications that reach far beyond these valleys . . ."

"The thing about the bees?"

"Not just. I met the person in charge of the Waldensian cultural center's library. You know, Torre Pellice is the capital of the Waldensian Church. At the advice of the booksellers at Claudiana Books I went to visit this Signor Miro, and we had a long talk . . ."

Just as she was about to add that he had invited her to dinner, she realized that the particulars of the menu escaped her. And besides, now wasn't the time to list them and provoke grumbling from Marco.

"What's the connection between the Waldensians and the murders at the beekeeper's house?"

"Well, let's just say that, generally speaking, the history of the Waldensians, who were heretics even before Protestantism . . ."

"OK, OK, there's no need to give me a lecture. I've read a few articles on the subject . . ."

Simona sighed.

"I'll just point out that, precisely because of their history, many Waldensians have maintained a certain soft spot for heretical behaviors and a love of debate. According to the booksellers, Miro was the person I needed to see, the most knowledgeable of them all when it comes to tensions in the valley around the question of the bees and modern agriculture. And they weren't wrong. Over the last several years there have been a lot of conferences, public debates held in piazzas and on television, town hall meetings addressing problems like GMOs and the disappearance of the bees, problems that concern the regional economy as much as the health of local residents. Miro didn't miss a single one. He showed me a stack of papers: essentially confidential convention programs and brochures for the audience. And he arrived at a pretty convincing conclusion. The people I thought were just lunatics at first, members of the valley's circle of technophiles, are actually part of a network of international influence, with a mission statement and everything, all financed by Sacropiano. It seems the company decided to turn this valley into a laboratory for experiments involving cutting-edge technologies—for example, perfecting new pesticides, modifying animal species, molecular engineering, and nanotechnology. And they're testing the limits of what's acceptable on the local population."

"Oh God, my poor little girl! What have you gotten yourself mixed up in? I hope the dinner was good, at least . . ."

"What dinner?"

Marco let out a little laugh.

"You don't expect me to believe that you had this conversation over a glass of water? I hear the way you're talking, sweetie, and I know what time you're calling me. You had a little feast, no? And after that, your Waldensian jumped your bones? And you wallowed in lust and fornication?"

"Stop talking nonsense."

Marco abandoned his jocular tone. "You ate out, didn't you? I called you at the hotel a little while ago. They told me they hadn't seen you all day."

"Yes, I stayed away to avoid the reporters, but my strategy didn't work with Ciuffani. That viper would have slept in the lobby all night just to head me off. You know, that guy is goddamn hand in glove with the Internal Information and Security Agency, I'm sure of it."

"Don't start up again with your paranoia about the secret service. And don't change the subject. Who did you have dinner with?"

"Oh, what's the big deal? Are you done acting like a jealous teenager? Yes, I had dinner with Signor Miro . . ."

She was about to add that he was seventy years old and paralyzed on one side of his body, but her mind suddenly returned to the menu, and in a fit of sadism she rattled it off for him. Marco listened in silence before spitting out venomously:

"Fine then, if after all of that he didn't manage to screw you, your Waldensian is really an idiot."

And he hung up.

*   *   *

First and foremost, acceptance is a matter of business sense: knowing what is acceptable and what is not, and what needs to be done in order for the public to accept a given technological development. This notion was born with the advent of the technologies we have seen emerge in recent decades, in particular genetic engineering (DNA, GMOs), information and communications technology (the Internet, telephone technology, radio frequency identification), biometrics, and even nanotechnology, which is still relatively new. Explosions in technological innovation lead to great social transformations as well as legitimate public health, social, and political concerns. We are confronted with the challenge of reorganizing the most basic aspects of the ties that bind us.

Another advancement occurred with the development of acceptance assessment techniques, which are methods of anticipating what the public will be able to handle. It's no longer a matter of needs or desires but rather of knowing what the average consumer and the nation at large will be unwilling to tolerate. Social acceptance is therefore a matter of rendering acceptable things that are unacceptable (or that go against certain values). Studies on social acceptance demonstrate a cynicism typical of the business world and, upon close inspection, reveal a certain political agenda. Recommendations published by national research centers, whether European Union or privately funded, are aimed above all at developing markets for new technologies, being as careful as possible to avoid any political, social, or cultural objections. Two European research commissions, the JRC (the Joint Research Centre) and the IPTS (the Institute for Prospective Technological Studies), set the tone.

This approach to managing desires reveals more than just the egoism of an obscure managerial class. How can we see it as anything other than a logical consequence of the prevailing economic system and social climate? Exposing the conspiracy would only lead to confusion. Social acceptance hinges on our society's endemic fascination with all things modern, new, and original. Due to a collective inability to come up with other sources of common ground, few escape this infatuation with new technologies.

Nevertheless, certain innovations remain shocking, and must be predigested in order for the public to tolerate them. This is often why public officials take up ethical issues: "It is possible that [. . .] in the future, competitive advantage will be determined by the ability to anticipate and cater to the tolerance of social phenomena, mechanisms of appropriation, and modes of expression." The motto that governs this research is "create participation to create acceptance." This consists in creating the illusion of objective information, which is reinforced by a series of mechanisms of cooperation with consumers and citizens. A period of maturation, also known as "co-conception" in research and development jargon, serves to take the "social temperature"; this is done through a series of debates, town hall meetings, conferences for circles of science enthusiasts, all supposedly independent of any economic interests.

Under the pretense of fostering collaboration with citizens and consumers, social acceptance is ultimately merely a strategy for diffusing opposition to certain technologies. If the words "ethical," "environment," and "safety" are frequently invoked, it is primarily to reassure investors and put their minds at ease. Signor Renzo Tomellini, head of the Department of Nanoscience and Nanotechnology at the European Commission Directorate-General for Research, articulates it clearly in a report for the French Senate in 2003: "I am not talking about a moral approach, but a utilitarian approach. Major investors [. . .] invest in sectors that are considered neutral or secure from an ecological or ethical standpoint. They want to avoid potential minefields like GMOs. In other words, they want to participate in responsible development: not just something that is ethically and morally correct, but also beneficial to the economy because it constitutes a secure investment. And investors need security."

Several opposition movements have already frightened public officials and industrial powers into learning their lesson not to introduce a new technology too quickly and too carelessly.

Simona felt her eyes closing on her.

Reading the pamphlet given to her by Signor Miro had helped her to calm down after the argument with her husband. She put it down and turned out the light.

Just before drifting off to sleep, a question suddenly arose in her mind: Exactly what were they trying to get the valley's inhabitants to accept? She tried not to look for an answer, but she tossed and turned for a long time before losing consciousness.

And as she was flailing around in her bed, three floors below, in the only armchair in Ciuffani's room, a man of about fifty was drinking his third glass of whiskey from a bottle he had procured for himself at the bar. The reporter, on the other hand, wearing a dressing gown and sitting on the edge of the double bed, was on his first drink. He gazed down at his Band-Aid-wrapped big toe with a sullen expression.

"That bitch really hurt me," he grumbled. "For tomorrow's episode of *La Mosca* I'll do a show live from San Giorgio al Monte and I'll really lay into her, the big whore . . . And to think that some people find her charming. My network director even used the word 'sexy.' Can you believe that? With that giant ass and white hair?"

The man in the armchair, bald and slightly overweight, wearing leather moccasins, linen pants, and a designer polo shirt, made a gesture with his hand as if swatting away a fly.

"*De gustibus* . . ." he murmured.

He seemed to be musing to himself and took a while to finish his whiskey before adding: "Far be it from me to give you orders, but I think that, for the moment, it would be better if you didn't attack her."

The reporter sneered.

"I'm sure you're not trying to put words in my mouth. I'll content myself to broadcast the information that the Internal Information and Security Agency brings me, provided it's something I find interesting. And you know very well that if you all try to coerce me into coverage that goes against my conscience, I'll be the first to denounce you to the public. Just because we share the same vision of Italy's future doesn't mean you get to treat me like your puppet. For instance, if I want to bury Tavianello tomorrow . . ."

The man from the AISI brought his hands up in front of him.

"Of course," he said with a warm smile. "We know that it's only out of patriotism that you defend our theories on the nation's most sensitive issues whenever we ask you to. And it's only in recognition of your high standard of patriotism that we wanted to bring some good real estate opportunities to your attention."

Then the intelligence agent's smile instantly disappeared.

"But we don't waste time with idle chitchat," he added. "You know as well as I do that you have no interest in attacking us; that would weaken you considerably, and maybe then we would no longer be able to stop certain jackals from disseminating certain videos . . . For example, the one where you're playing Polanski with a minor in a hot tub . . ."

Ciuffani went pale. He returned his injured foot to the ground. A shudder shot through the long, muscular legs, left bare by the open dressing gown.

"What are you saying?" he croaked.

The agent smiled again.

"Come on, Ciuffani. Nothing to be afraid of. We're friends, aren't we?"

The reporter ran a hand through his unkempt hair.

"I didn't know she was a minor . . . It's not the kind of thing that would have come up . . ."

The agent shook his head.

"Yes, that's what Polanski said in his defense, and we have no reason to doubt your word," he remarked, placing his glass on the nightstand and rising to his feet. "Let's forget this nonsense. You will not attack Tavianello tomorrow night for the simple reason that it would be the wrong move. We'll be keeping an eye on her. For now, my advice would be to drop just a few of those vicious insinuations that you've developed such a talent for. For example, you could say that it's surprising how antimafia experts refuse to take terrorism investigations seriously. We'll wait for Tavianello to go all in, and then I promise you we'll have her hide. You know that she's stepped on our toes enough times, too.

"This whole 'Worker Bee Revolution' thing reeks of radical environmentalism. A prominent French intellectual, I can't remember who . . . Bernard-Henri Lévy maybe, or no, it was a woman . . . whoever it was said that radicalism is often the shortest path to stupidity. An important slogan for us extremists of moderation, don't you think? This time, a little radical ecological terrorism could be the shortest path to eliminating any opposition to Sacropiano's major research project in these valleys, a project our government is very invested in. I'll tell you about it some other time. And if Tavianello goes off course, as we hope she will, we'll be able to kill two birds with one stone."

As he said this, he walked to the door, placing his hand on the knob. He held up the bottle of whiskey he had in his hand.

"I'll take this with me. I'm guessing that great marathon runners abstain from heavy drinking, am I right?"

Ciuffani made a weary gesture and said nothing.

"At any rate, I still have some work to do," the agent sighed. "I need fuel."

* * *

An hour later, in the plains surrounding Pinerolo, a small white van was driving on a dirt path. Jostling violently, it drove along a line of poplars, forded a stream, and came out on a narrow paved road. On either side, a nearly full moon shone on fields surrounded by netting, propped up by white signs among the plants. The road curved left and continued parallel to a metal fence, to which a No TRESPASSING sign was affixed every three hundred feet, bearing underneath the name of a multinational agro-chemical corporation. After driving about a half a mile the van stopped.

The driver turned around to face the passenger.

"Are you sure the alarm has been deactivated?"

"Of course I'm sure. The security company is under our control."

The two men got out of the van, the passenger carrying with him a large bag. They jumped over a trickling stream and found themselves standing inches from the chain-link fence.

The passenger pulled a pair of long diagonal pliers from the bag. He handed them to the driver.

"Why me?" said the latter.

His interlocutor sneered back at him.

"I have to finish this," he said, pulling a bottle of whiskey from the bag, and as the other man cut the wire, he downed the last of it.

CHAPTER 6

*T*HE BUILDING RESEMBLED A TYPICAL enormous warehouse, with the sort of bare cement walls that one sees on
the outskirts of almost every city in the world of the rich: one
hundred feet tall and five hundred feet long, standing over a
sweeping expanse of cultivated plants divided into lots, their
numbers indicated by various signs. It was the kind of work
of human genius that made Simona feel like going back to
feeding her stray cats under the Sublician Bridge in Rome,
at the heart of a city that was still a city. In the large parking lot in front of another building, police vehicles could
be distinguished from those of the employees by their hap-
hazard parking jobs, having been left wherever their drivers
had found space. In front of the tall sliding doors the white
jumpsuits from Forensics were going about their work.
Farther along on the right, the minesweepers were keeping
busy, some removing their reinforced jumpsuits, composite

helmets, and polycarbonate visors, while those without the necessary attire hoisted a robot up on top of the van. On the opposite side, their arms crossed, Evangelisti and Calabonda watched in silence. When they saw her arrive, the former smiled and the latter shook his head.

"So you still think terrorism should be disregarded in the investigation?" the prosecutor asked her when she was a few steps away.

He gestured toward the wall next to the doors, where three-foot-tall letters written in spray paint said: SACROPIANO KILLS. THE WORKER BEE REVOLUTION LIVES.

"What was it?"

"An improvised explosive device," the maresciallo said matter-of-factly. "Like in Iraq. A gas cylinder paired with two cans of gasoline and a detonator stolen from the army as a focalization device . . ."

"Stolen from or provided by . . ." murmured Simona.

"Excuse me?" said Evangelisti.

"No, nothing. Why didn't it explode?"

"The bomb disposal team says the detonator was defective."

"And there was no alarm, no video surveillance system, no guards positioned around the warehouse?"

Calabonda shrugged.

"As you saw, there's a security booth at the entrance equipped with video surveillance. Except that last night at four forty-five, after a virus was introduced into the computer system, the monitors started playing previously recorded footage in a loop rather than continuing to show what was happening in real time. We found the point where the terrorists entered. Around five o'clock they cut the wire fencing, and they acted while the cameras were down. You'd have to be a damn expert to access the security computer system. But we'll verify that. If there was any negligence or complicity involved, we'll find out about it sooner or later . . ."

Simona sighed.

"Let's hope so. What is manufactured in this building?"

"That would be a question for its owner," Evangelisti replied, pointing to a luxury car with tinted windows that was pulling into a reserved space.

From it emerged a man in full executive attire: suit and tie, an expensive watch that could be seen from a mile away, stylish glasses, confident stride.

With a few steps, he reached the group.

"So," he asked Evangelisti, not wasting any time on hellos. "Do you have any leads?"

"Allow me to introduce Francesco Signorelli, executive director of the Sacropiano Center for Research in Pinerolo," the prosecutor said to Simona.

Signorelli forced a big, unfriendly smile and held out his hand. "Ah, you must be the famous Commissario Tavianello? Come to lend a hand to our esteemed maresciallo?"

With a nervous finger, Calabonda pushed his glasses up on his nose and cleared his throat. "In an officious capacity," he ventured.

"Absolutely officious," said the commissario. "The fact that I allowed my gun to be stolen and that it was then used to kill your engineer hardly makes me especially qualified."

The director chuckled.

"I read a similar appraisal in an interview with Ciuffani that came out in my brother's newspaper this morning . . ."

"Your brother?"

"Yes, my dear older brother. Alberto directs the *Quotidiano delle Valli*. And don't think that it benefits my business. He gives too much space to opponents of progress in general and of our laboratories in particular for my tastes . . . but if I may ask, I'd like to know where we are with the investigation," he finished, turning to face Calabonda and Evangelisti.

"In the preliminary stages," the magistrate responded, visibly irritated by the executive's manner. "But Commissario Tavianello was just asking me what is produced in your laboratory."

Francesco Signorelli smoothed his tie, glanced at his watch, and crossed his arms.

"Oh, 'produce' isn't quite the word. We conduct research on the agro-industrial applications of different types of nanotechnology. Do you have some idea as to what that means?" he asked with a wry smile.

"Of course," said Simona, to whom the question had been addressed. "Every now and again I manage to read something aside from memos. So-called nanotechnologies are methods of altering matter at an atomic and molecular level, which allows or which will allow—I don't quite know—the atom-for-atom manufacturing of infinitesimal tools, artificial microorganisms, nanorobots. There has been talk of nanorobots capable of reproduction, which has raised fears of catastrophic scenarios. Michael Crichton wrote a book about it . . ."

The executive brought his hands together in a gesture of prayer, as though to invoke the spirit of progress and science.

"Every new advancement in knowledge causes irrational fears," he declared. "It's human nature, don't you think?"

Simona abstained not only from responding but from expressing any thought whatsoever. When a singer tried to get the audience to sing along to a chorus at a concert, when a supervisor posed a question to the auditorium at a work assembly, when a speaker at a political or union rally threw out a slogan for the crowd to repeat, her reaction was always the same: she slumped her shoulders and waited for the moment to pass. This behavior dated back to her youth, when she was subjected to the teaching methods of an elementary school instructor who never finished her sentences but rather waited for the pupils to complete them, while Simona, a child trying to find the right words, thought, *It's your sentence—figure it out yourself!*

"What do you think?" repeated Signorelli. When no one said anything, he continued: "We're on the verge of developing a new generation of pesticides that will have the capacity to penetrate on a nanometric scale—meaning a millionth of a millimeter," he benevolently clarified for Calabonda, whose creased forehead expressed confusion. "Because these products will be far more powerful than the ones currently available, they will be effective in infinitely smaller amounts. Do you understand what that means?"

When no one indicated that they understood, he explained:

"It means that it will be much, much more ecological. Do you understand?" he repeated, with a little smile directed at Calabonda.

Simona observed the maresciallo, his arms crossed, perplexed, silent. His whole body had contracted as though to absorb the contempt that evidently rained down on him in this region and to which the rich, powerful so-and-so Signorelli delicately paid tribute. A faint feeling of compassion began to stir in her, but then the carabiniere slowly removed his sunglasses, smoothed his mustache, and asked:

"But aren't these nanoparticles at risk of crossing the blood-brain barrier?"

Francesco Signorelli's mouth dropped open and he stammered, "The blood . . . the blood . . ."

"Yes, the blood-brain barrier that separates the circulating blood from the central nervous system of every living being on earth, protecting it against toxins and hormones circulating in the bloodstream. If the nanoparticles that make up your pesticides are capable of flowing directly into the brain, won't that cause massive damage to humans and animals alike?"

When the executive just stared back at him, speechless, Calabonda added, "You seem stunned by my question. But it's my duty as an officer to read the literature produced by the militant environmentalists who oppose you—to better protect you, you understand."

Seeing as the honorable Dottore Signorelli's silence continued, the maresciallo added, "Carabinieri know how to use Wikipedia, too."

Calabonda returned his glasses to his face and the executive let out a faint laugh of appreciation.

"My compliments, Maresciallo. No, obviously creating a product that would endanger human and animal health is out of the question. We are only trying to fight the parasites that threaten our crops as effectively as possible."

The carabiniere pointed to the gigantic building behind him with his thumb.

"Can we take a look inside?" he asked. But Signorelli shook his head.

"Ah, that's completely impossible. Our research is highly confidential and the findings are systematically protected by patent law. Please understand—competition is fierce in our sector. There are countless attempts at corporate espionage, and the orders from our global board of directors are extremely strict. Without a search warrant, access to company property is severely limited."

There was a pause. Calabonda didn't say anything. Nor did Evangelisti. Simona took him by the arm.

"May I speak with you?"

They took a few steps away from the others.

"Why don't you ask for a warrant to search the company's properties?" she asked.

Evangelisti passed his large hand over his small head.

"What would that accomplish? Pending evidence to the contrary, the company is the victim, no?"

"Yes, but, for whatever reason, members of their staff could be involved. The computer failure that deactivated the surveillance cameras—don't you think that suggests that it could have been partly an inside job? We'd need to see their list of personnel, take a look inside their lockers, see if the explosive device could have been assembled in the same laboratory . . ."

Evangelisti shook his head.

"This center is protected by a special statute. Before making any move having to do with it, I have to call Turin and request approval from my superiors, who refer the matter to Rome. You see, the research conducted here is of national importance. And on a side note, just between the two of us, the Signorelli brothers are members of the prime minister's party, and they have some very powerful political and institutional supporters. So if I seek authorization to search the premises now I'm sure I won't get it. I don't have enough to back up such a request."

Simona and the prosecutor walked back to where the executive stood. Lifting his long arm toward the graffiti, the magistrate asked him, "Is there anything in your current operations that could explain this slogan?"

Signorelli shook his head. "You can't know what's going on inside people's heads. Those guys from the Alpine Valley Beekeepers' Defense League say that colony collapse disorder is caused by our pesticides, but it's never been proven. We think that it has to do with parasites like the Varroa destructor or viruses like IAPV or the bubonic plague. We are 100 percent prepared to conduct research in collaboration with the apiculturists, but they prefer to resort to tactics of pure aggression, sabotaging the debates and meetings that we organize . . ."

"Do you believe this attempt could have been made by the League?" Calabonda broke in.

The executive made a skeptical face.

"Maybe not the League itself, but every movement has its extremists. I'm not formally accusing anyone. Still, that Minoncelli is a damned hothead . . ."

"We'll make all the necessary inquiries," the maresciallo said.

"I have no doubt," the executive affirmed. He gestured toward the building's large doors. "Now if you don't need anything further from me, I have to begin what is sure to be a long day of work. Of course, let it be understood that I am at your disposal."

He reached out to shake the carabiniere's hand.

"I'm sure that you will find the perpetrators quickly, Maresciallo. And compliments on your scientific knowledge. You really impressed me," he concluded, with a faint note of superiority that made Simona want to slap him.

The black hairs of the carabiniere's mustache quivered as he shook the outstretched hand and mumbled, "You can count on us. We'll investigate all possible theories."

"Except for the insurance scam angle, of course," Simona said jokingly, holding out her hand to receive her handshake.

Signorelli forced a weak laugh. Out of the corner of her eye, the commissario glimpsed an expression on Calabonda's face that she hadn't seen before: one of amusement. After he had shaken hands with Evangelisti as well, the executive walked purposefully toward the entrance.

Calabonda removed his sunglasses for the second time. *And to think*, thought Simona, *to an outside observer, it might look like nothing out of the ordinary is happening!*

"Commissario," began the maresciallo, clearing his throat. "I still haven't thanked you for your intervention yesterday, during Berisha's arrest. Without you I would have found myself in a very difficult situation."

"Oh, don't give it another thought," said Simona.

"Actually, yes, I intend to. I'm planning to write to the newspapers to contest the version of the story that Ciuffani is about to put forward."

"Please—let it go. I'm used to media controversies. They fizzle out on their own, especially when no one fans the flames. Rather, tell me: How is Berisha?"

"Apparently still in the hospital. The doctors say his life isn't in danger, even though he lost a lot of blood. According to Doctor Pasquano, the caliber of the bullet that shattered his knee is the same as the bullet that killed Mauro Danela, the beekeeper who went to destroy Minoncelli's apiary. By the way, were you able to read my report?"

Simona shot a look at Evangelisti. She didn't know whether the magistrate had told the carabiniere he'd keep her up to date on the case's progress, but she decided to lay her cards on the table.

"Yes, Evangelisti brought me a copy this morning at the hotel. I only had time to glance at it before he called me to let me know what had happened here. But from what I read, it seems that Danela and Minoncelli were enemies, that he had a serious problem with the fact that he used foreign bees, from Slovenia, or Borneo, or I don't know where. He said that this bastardized the pure Italian species."

"Yes, that might explain why he took advantage of Minoncelli's compulsory stay with us to go and destroy his apiary. But as far as his death is concerned, we're totally in the dark. The same goes for who shot Berisha. The thing with the military-style weaponry is very unsettling . . . and if it's part of a 'Worker Bee Revolution' counterstrike, the ecoterrorism angle is definitely worth exploring . . ."

"And what about Bertolazzi's death? I didn't have time to read the report."

"We strongly suspect Berisha. I have numerous witnesses who saw him at Minoncelli's house at the time of the murder. They're keeping him under watch at the hospital until he can be interrogated. His fingerprints are being compared to the ones found on the weapon—aside from yours, obviously—and I'm waiting for the results."

After saying good-bye to the maresciallo, the commissario and the prosecutor walked side by side to their respective cars, which were parked at the other end of the lot.

After a few steps, Simona asked, "What gaffes did Calabonda make to prompt people to come up with the term 'to pull a Cacabonda'?"

"Our maresciallo surprised you, eh? You're thinking he might not be as stupid as he seems. And you're not wrong. Let's just say that he has an extremely rigid sense of his duties and he had trouble adapting to the ways of the valley. For example, he decided to check drivers' blood alcohol levels right as they were leaving a *plaisentif* festival— that's one of our typical cheeses. I don't know whether you're familiar with it, but it makes you thirsty . . . The majority of the population saw this as an attack on local custom."

"I see."

"That's not the worst of it. We had a strike at a dairy plant. The situation was very tense; the workers threatened to take an executive hostage, like in France. Calabonda plunked down a cordon of men at the entrance, but when one man tried to get through the blockade, Calabonda didn't believe he was who he said he was. He took him for an agitator and he clocked him with his billy club. The man turned out to be the mayor, come to talk to the workers.

Fortunately the mayor didn't want to press charges, but long story short, word got around the valleys . . ."

"Your maresciallo is a complex character."

The magistrate stopped to look at the commissario. Simona made out a pair of intense, penetrating eyes in that face, totally swallowed up by the beard and topped off by that tuft of uncombed hair.

"We're all complex characters, it seems to me," he observed. "We all have our dark spots. You, for example . . ."

"Yes?"

"Well . . . don't take offense . . . I'm happy that you are following the investigation up close. But on some level I wonder why you're so intent on staying here when you could easily be spending your vacation in Sicily."

Simona unlocked the car doors with her remote before answering.

"First of all I don't like—truly do not like at all—the fact that they stole my weapon to kill a man. And also . . ."

"Also?"

"Also . . . nothing," she said. "I think that's reason enough, don't you?"

"Certainly."

Later, as she was driving toward San Giorgio al Monte, she thought back to what had kept her from telling the magistrate the second reason she felt compelled to stay: the impression, as she'd already confided in Marco, that "something important" was happening in those mountains. The thought that had held her back was this:

How did Evangelisti know that Marco was waiting for her in Sicily? Was she being watched? And if so, by whom?

*   *   *

As she entered the nameless café on the outskirts of town where she had met him the previous morning, Simona wasn't surprised to see Giuseppe Felice, sitting in the same spot, writing on a small laptop. He was so absorbed in what he was doing that he didn't hear her come up behind him, and when she placed a hand on his shoulder he jumped violently. Then, turning around, he saw her, and he had a surprising reaction: he bent his arm and held it up in front of his face, like a child afraid of being slapped.

"I'm sorry," he said, immediately lowering his arm. "But my editorial director demanded an interview, and you didn't want to give me one—"

"What are you talking about?"

With his chin, Felice gestured toward the newspaper display stand on the counter, where a bold headline appeared on the front page: Bruno Ciuffani's denunciation of "Tavianello's Dubious Role in the San Giorgio al Monte Multiple Homicide Investigation: Exclusive Interview."

Simona shrugged.

"It doesn't matter," she said. "That's the job. You know what they say: there are no stupid people, only stupid professions. So, did the neural network software work?" she inquired, taking a seat across from the reporter.

He shook his head "no" and assumed a pitiful expression.

"Not a chance. It completely froze my computer. I spent an hour trying to get it to work again."

Simona ordered a coffee and waited for it in silence. Ill at ease, Felice fidgeted in his chair, then motioned to close his computer. The commissario stopped him.

"Wait. The photos taken at the crime scene—are they on this computer, or did you use your software to delete them?"

"No, there're still on here."

"Can I look at them?"

"Right now?"

"Yes. Let me see."

She moved her chair to position herself next to the reporter. When the coffee shop owner brought her coffee he found the plump white-haired signora and the little redheaded fellow sitting snugly shoulder to shoulder, their heads tilted toward each other as they both looked at the screen. The barista made a face that conveyed both perplexity and an infinite tolerance for his fellow creatures' perverse behavior. He set the cup down and left.

"Wait," Simona said at one point. "Can you go back to the last photo? Yes, that's the one."

She took a moment to study the image. Then she looked up at the reporter and, seeing that his computer was connected to the Internet, she asked him, "If I gave you my email address, would you send me these photos?

I promise you that you'll be the first to know if they lead to any interesting developments."

"You really think there could be something interesting in them?"

"Yes," she answered, distracted by the arrival of a tall, tan, muscular man with curly blond hair and light blue eyes.

"Tell me, is that Minoncelli by chance?" she asked, using her eyes to indicate the newcomer, who had just leaned against the bar and ordered a *caffè corretto*.

Felice looked up.

"Yes, that's him."

"Send me those photos?" she asked, getting up. "Write down your cell number for me. I'll get in touch with you very soon."

The reporter nodded. Simona was already walking toward the counter. Minoncelli recognized her and smiled.

"Look," he said, "our modest trattoria has turned into a celebrity hot spot."

The commissario gave him her hand to shake.

"It seems to me you're the celebrity here."

The man's handshake was sincere and straightforward, like his pale blue gaze (and don't pass judgment on this bit of romance-novel-style sentimentality, dear reader, because it's perfectly suited to that sweetness so genuine that it caused a lump in Simona's throat).

"Would you have a minute to give me some information? Strictly off the record, to be clear. You have every right to say no and I'd understand—"

The smile widened, revealing some of his perfect teeth.

"Are you always so courteous with the people you investigate?" he asked. "I'm guessing that you play the role of the good cop during interrogations, while a colleague plays the bad one . . ."

"I'm not investigating you."

"What are you doing, then? Aside from leaving a gun lying around that was used to kill that poor Bertolazzi at my home."

Simona ran all five of her fingers through her white mane.

"I'm trying to make sense of things," she said. "Trying to make sense of the recent series of events in this valley, because I have a feeling they concern more than just its inhabitants. It's only an intuition, but I believe that what's happening here concerns everyone in the country, if not in the world."

"No kidding," said the beekeeper, whose unbroken gaze continued to study her. He let several seconds pass before adding, "Well, you're not wrong."

He emptied his cup, set a coin down on the counter, looked at his watch.

"There's something I have to do in the city, but if you want, we can meet back here in two hours. I have to go work in another apiary a couple of miles from here."

* * *

Standing squarely on his feet, Maresciallo Calabonda straightened his sunglasses on his nose until the arcs of his eyebrows disappeared, creating a certain resemblance between his face and the head of an insect. Then he crossed his arms. In front of him the burly, ponytailed man who directed the center's security team shifted his feet, wiped away the beads of sweat that had gathered on his forehead, and cleared his throat.

"All right," said the carabiniere, pointing to the series of monitors behind them, "you're telling me that these screens are all hooked up to a single computer, located in this room . . ."

Without turning his head or uncrossing his arms, he stuck his right index finger out over his left elbow to indicate the machine sitting on the desk to the security director's right. The man drew his head back between his shoulders slightly, which made the folds in the back of his neck that much more pronounced.

". . . and that this computer isn't connected to the outside?" finished the carabiniere.

The head of security nodded, his ponytail swaying above the collar of his blue uniform shirt.

"That's right," he admitted in an unsteady voice.

"Then how do you explain the fact that your video surveillance system broke down right as these individuals infiltrated the center's perimeter?"

The man sighed heavily.

"Clearly it was an act of sabotage. But . . ."

And he went quiet.

Calabonda smoothed his mustache.

"But what?"

"But if I were in your place—"

"You are *not* in my place," the carabiniere said curtly. "Tell me what you have to say."

"Well, I'm not sure that one should necessarily jump to the conclusion that there were inside collaborators. I've already interrogated members of my staff. One of them confessed to having installed a video game on the computer from a flash drive. For passing the time during surveillance shifts . . ."

"What?"

The head guard brought his hand up.

"It's a serious thing, and I told him that when our internal investigation was finished he'd be suspended until a penalty could be determined. In any event, it's possible that game jammed the entire system unintentionally."

"Unintentionally? You mean to tell me it's a coincidence that a terrorist ambush and the breakdown of the security system occurred simultaneously?"

"You know, the system was down for four hours and the terrorists couldn't have been on the premises for more than one."

Calabonda shook his head.

"I'm not convinced. Not in the least. You're coming with me to headquarters, with your man—the one who downloaded the game to the computer. We'll have time to go over the facts again."

The walkie-talkie in the maresciallo's belt crackled. He brought the device to his ear, listened for several seconds, and mumbled: "Get over there." Then he got back to the watchman.

"You're going to leave one of your men here and have him show three of my men how the surveillance system is secured. Go wait for me by our cars, along with the genius who downloaded that little game. And tell him to bring the flash drive, if he hasn't already gotten rid of it."

As Brigadier Lagazo crossed the threshold to enter, he passed the head watchman on his way out, his head down with an air of mortification.

"Not the sharpest tool in the shed," the maresciallo mumbled. "So, what do you have to tell me that's so urgent?"

The brigadier reached out to show him a plastic bag.

"A very interesting piece of evidence."

Drawing near it, Calabonda opened it from above and saw its contents.

"A bottle of whiskey? What's interesting about that?"

"We found it in a bush not far from the place where the fence was cut," the brigadier declared. "And it's not just any bottle of whiskey."

Seeing his triumphant expression, Calabonda, who had had a feeling he was being taken for a ride from the moment he'd arrived at the research center, began to hope.

* * *

Marco Tavianello scooped up the last remains of almond granita with a long spoon. Then he picked up the last crumb of brioche with one finger and cleaned his hands with a paper napkin, raising his eyes to watch the fashion show consisting of men in Bermuda shorts and women covered in brightly colored transparent sarongs. He asked himself yet again whether the human species could really be made up of such beings. From that café patio on the island of Salina, the view of the stretch of sea separating them from the island of Lipari was full of the bustling movements of a species of anthropoids that to his mind could not have a place on the same branch of the evolutionary tree to which he himself felt he belonged. It wasn't just the droves of Milanese that gave him, a Neapolitan, this sensation, even though their mad obsession with building hot-tub-equipped mansions in the middle of the Mediterranean shrubland struck him as potentially extraterrestrial behavior. It was more the things they were talking about, the way they spoke, the way they laughed, their gestures—all of it was so foreign to him that he felt the sudden urge to call Simona.

He sighed, took his cell phone from the pocket of his long linen pants, hesitated several seconds as he looked at the number, then made up his mind.

"The person you are trying to call is unreachable. . . ."

What the fuck! He ended the call. What was Simona doing up there, anyway?

* * *

Climbing up the narrow roads of a mountain village, walking among patches of blinding sunlight and soft shadows, smells of basil, of pine, of cat piss, of mold and damp and heavy roses. Catching sight of something under a caryatid, something so strikingly white that you can't tell whether it's a bedsheet beside you or a blanket of snow overhead, up on the peaks that dominate the horizon. Smelling the coldness of the water even before feeling it on your skin. Thrusting both hands into an icy fountain.

Finding yourself without looking for yourself, after catching your breath, in a shadowy corner between the cold stone and the burning sun, fully aware that nobody knows where you are.

Unreachable. What an ugly word for such a beautiful moment.

Simona had turned off her cell phone and was in an inexpressibly good mood. On the far end of the little piazza, in one of the high-up neighborhoods of San Giorgio al Monte, she was sitting on some greenish fountain steps bathed in bright sunlight. She savored a long moment of peace before deciding to knock on a metal door, which was painted green and set in a wall that connected two stone buildings.

"Come in," said a voice. "It's open."

She turned the handle and pushed the door open. The contrast between the naked stone of the piazza and the profuse vegetation that now met her eyes reminded her of crossing over from the desert to an oasis during a trip she and Marco had made to southern Tunisia, and the rapture they had both felt as they entered it.

On the left there was an enormous bellflower plant, from which protruded stalks more than three feet long and laden with white and lilac-colored clusters. To the right an array of bugles, wood sorrels, foxgloves, and devil's nettle formed distinct layers of silvery green, wine red, white, pink, purple, blue, and turquoise in a profusion of round, tubular, trumpet-shaped, and climbing flowers. At the end of a path bordered by jasmine plants whose perfume wafted several inches above her head was a rose-covered lattice. Underneath it Professor Martini gestured with his left hand for her to come closer, his face turned to the right. The air hummed with infinite buzzing sounds. Simona walked toward the professor. When she reached him she noticed a bee resting on his speckled hand, surrounded by the sweet smells of the yellow and purple roses that bloomed cheek to jowl.

"An *Osmia cornuta*," he said. "You see this white tuft on the head? It's a male. In this species, the female has the horns."

The bee flew away and he looked up at the commissario.

"That's not the only trait that distinguishes this species from the bees we keep to produce honey," he said smiling. "Unlike the *Apis mellifera* and other domesticated species, wild bees are solitary, not social. Which is why one can easily draw the conclusion that domestication and exploitation are directly responsible for the very existence of any society. Would you care for some tea? Or coffee? A glass of water?"

Simona shook her head.

"Thank you, but I don't need anything. I just quenched my thirst at that magnificent fountain in the piazza."

"Then you must have ingested excessive amounts of saltpeter. I set up tubs of filtered water for my pets," he said, gesturing toward the shimmering liquid at the foot of a hydrangea whose flowers were as large as babies' heads. "But please, sit down."

They settled into two weathered painted folding chairs. Martini placed his right hand on a round metal table with a mesh-pattern top. Simona realized that what she had mistaken for liver spots or birthmarks were in fact droplets of honey.

"Look," said the scientist, gesturing toward the insect on his hand with his chin. "The magnificent metallic sheen, the black belly . . . It's an *Osmia caerulescens*. You usually only find these around the wisteria over there by the wall. They love leguminous plants . . ."

Out of nowhere yet another insect came and landed on his hand, then set to work on one of the golden splotches.

"Ah, this is a nice surprise!" Martini exclaimed excitedly. "There shouldn't be any of these left . . . It's a

Chelostoma florisomne, and my buttercups bloomed a while ago. But it's definitely her; the yellow belly can't trick us."

Another creature joined the others on his hand and prepared to suck up the honey.

"Meet *Osmia adunca*, who generally feeds from Viper's Bugloss, which I have a bed of behind the hydrangeas. Well, as you can see, it also enjoys my homemade nectar. Now we have two *Megachile willughbiella*, which closely resemble the honeybee aside from the black stripes on their abdomens. And here is *Eucera longicornis* . . . In the two years I've been here I've documented seventy wild bee species in my garden. I started feeding them with a nectar I make myself, completely organic and free of any pesticides, of course."

He raised the hand on which a half dozen insects were now gathering nectar.

"This way I can extend their life spans in many cases . . . Their natural food source, which can be a specific plant or plant species, usually only lasts a few weeks."

"Is this your way of combating the bees' disappearance? Are you in the process of domesticating new species?" Simona asked.

"God forbid! I think domestication is possibly the worst thing to have happened to the honeybee and its kind. Let's just say I'm trying to foster a new kind of relationship between them and us. It's part of a project that you will most likely find megalomaniacal, but it's the last hope for human survival. A new kind of alliance between living beings in which mankind is no longer at the center, but rather one component out of many . . . A vain hope, don't you think?"

He sighed ironically.

Simona inhaled, exhaled, and watched the bees on the man's hand gorge themselves on nectar.

There was a moment of silence. In that garden, vast as the dark of night and as the light of day, perfumes, sounds, and colors corresponded.

Then, one by one, the bees took flight from the professor's hand, and Simona went back to being a cop.

"You didn't answer the question I asked you the other day. Why did the bees disappear from Minoncelli's apiary? Were they traumatized by the attack on their hives? And if so, why would *all* of them leave? It's rather strange that a few groups wouldn't stay behind, or even just one . . . You'd almost think they emigrated out of the blue."

"I was right," he said spiritedly. "You've already understood everything. But you still don't know what it means," he added, as a shadow of sadness passed over his eyes. Then he told Simona about the damage caused by pesticides, how they weakened bees' immune systems as much as those of humans, about the trauma it caused to transport them, about the deplorable conditions hundreds of thousands of transhumant beehives were subjected to in the United States in order to improve commercial almond production. He also told her about the theory that pheromones emitted by the bees could influence human psychology, and that the afflictions of a few individuals could have consequences for others, which would explain, he concluded, ". . . why there are so many crazy people in these valleys, including me."

He talked about a lot of things. But as she was pushing the metal door open to leave, Simona took one last look at him. She regarded the bald cranium bent over the hand where he'd drizzled a few drops of nectar, the hunched-over, lanky, mantis-like body under the pergola, and she felt as though he had really been talking to her about something else entirely. Something that went well beyond the crucial point they had touched on so briefly.

*   *   *

Due to the arrival of a busful of Bavarian tourists, the noise in the hotel lobby was deafening. Calabonda had to lean over the small table in order to be understood by Ciuffani without yelling.

"Thank you for agreeing to answer some of my questions, Signore. To unravel a baffling case like this one we need the help of everyone who is willing and kind enough to cooperate."

"I'm always on the side of the law," Ciuffani said, glancing at himself in the large mirror on the wall near the corner sofa where they were sitting. "You know that I have a special bond with the carabinieri," he went on, sweeping his hair back. "Go ahead. I'm ready to answer all of your questions."

"All right then," said the maresciallo. "I'm sure you'll be able to explain what this was doing near the wire fence at Sacropiano's research center in Pinerolo, at the exact spot where it was apparently cut by the terrorists who carried out the failed attack. I'm sure you're up to speed on the attempt . . ."

"Of course . . . What is it?"

Ciuffani took the sealed envelope in his hand. It contained an empty bottle of whiskey.

"This bottle has a tiny tracking device under the label," said Calabonda. "See? There, in the corner. Well, one of my men recognized it immediately, having personally advised the management in this hotel to put them there after they realized that bottles stolen from local retailers were being trafficked through the company's supplies. That's how we were able to know with absolute certainty that this bottle was purchased yesterday evening at the bar in this hotel, by a man who then joined you in your room, where the two of you had, according to staff on that floor, a rather long meeting. Who was that man?"

The reporter's expression slowly changed as the carabiniere spoke. He took another look at himself in the mirror. He didn't recognize the panicked face that it reflected.

"Listen," he said, with a strained little laugh. "It's that . . . I . . . can't answer that question. I have to consult with . . . May I make a phone call? It's very urgent," he assured Calabonda as he stood up.

Calabonda shrugged his shoulders and forced a smile.

"Go on. You are free to come and go as you please."

"For now," he said under his breath as he watched the man take a few steps away and pull out his cell phone.

* * *

About an hour later, as the beekeeper's old jeep struggled to make the steep hairpin turns in the middle of the fir forest, Simona asked Minoncelli, "Have you already heard this whole thing about bee pheromones having the potential to influence people?"

Right then the vehicle went over a series of bumps, cracks, and potholes. The road horseshoed around, the steering wheel quivered in Minoncelli's hands, the incline got steeper. He fiddled with the gear stick and the accelerator. Several long minutes passed before he was able to respond.

"You spoke with Martini, right? I'd say it's not an entirely unfounded theory . . ."

The vehicle slowed and stopped. The beekeeper turned his arctic-lake-colored eyes on Simona.

"Listen," he said. "Breathe and listen."

Behind him, on the other side of the glass, she was able to make out, between the trunks of the larches, the mass of rhododendrons, their flowers like flaming crimson in the dark forest, and along the edges was the blond stain of the beehives. He opened the door of the jeep and got out, without taking his eyes off them.

"*Listen*," he repeated.

She heard the buzzing. Sweet, gentle, constant, endless. A faint, indescribable feeling—and something else. Perhaps the pheromones everyone had been talking about. The combination washed over her body like a long, interminable, maddening caress.

Minoncelli got to work.

* * *

That night, lying down in her room, Commissario Simona Tavianello told Marco about the man's gentle movements as he removed the slatted racks and adjusted the frames dripping with golden honey: the movement of the uncapping knife, the elegant way he offered his bare skin to the thousands of little darts without it being pierced by even one of them. She described it all in such rich detail that when she suddenly realized what she was doing, she immediately stopped talking.

Simona waited for her husband to get semi-hysterical and make some biting, jealous remark. But that's not what happened at all.

There was a brief silence. Then Marco simply said, "Listen, Simona, I'm just so bored here without you. Tomorrow I'm going to take the ferry back to Naples. I'll be in San Giorgio al Monte again by the afternoon. That is, if you want me there, of course," he added with a weak, nervous laugh.

"Are you joking? I'm thrilled! I just don't want to force you . . ."

"I'll be there. Goodnight, my darling."

He hung up. Simona stared at the receiver for several long seconds. She turned off the night-light and curled up in her bed. Her thoughts returned to Minoncelli's eyes. She wondered if she'd told her husband about them, those eyes.

A few seconds later, the hidden microphones planted in the room by the AISI recorded a muffled laugh, whose significance the senior officials were left to speculate on the following day.

CHAPTER 7

SIMONA WAS HAVING A DREAM ABOUT HELICOPTERS. The pilot turned to give her a thumbs-up: it was Professor Martini. She realized that with his frenzied expression and movements, the tall, scrawny, wild-haired carcass stooped over the aircraft's control stick bore a striking resemblance to Evangelisti. As she fought off a bout of nausea, she looked up at the blades, which had been replaced by swarms of innumerable insects. The aircraft was being carried by millions of bees fleeing their apiary.

The commissario opened her eyes. It looked like midday, but a glance at the digital alarm clock on the bedside table told her that it was only five thirty. The rumbling sound from her dream continued.

She got up, walked over to the window, pulled back the curtain. The view of the valley was superb. The dawn sky very pale, almost white. Between the hotel and the snow-covered mountains, made pink by the rising sun, were droves of helicopters.

The phone rang.

"Operation Edelweiss is underway," announced the tense voice of Evangelisti. "We're about to deal a major blow to ecoterrorism. If you want a front-row seat, meet us in the piazza in fifteen minutes."

Simona disliked—in fact, hated—rushing out the door without having a leisurely breakfast first. On the mornings of coordinated attacks she would rather get up at four thirty in the morning than give up the espresso-and-biscotti ritual that accompanied the gradual reawakening of her synapses. As she arrived in the main piazza her bad mood was compounded when she saw the vans of several television crews, both Italian and international, equipped with enormous parabolic antennae. There were at least a half dozen of them occupying the sidewalks and half of the street. At the far end of the piazza, behind a statue of Garibaldi, she recognized the black vehicles of the NOCS, the Italian antiterrorism unit, and spotted the balaclava-masked figures. Between her and them there was a small group of reporters—then there was a throng of uniforms. Walking toward them, she had to show her identification card, first at the barricade that held back the sea of video cameras, microphones, photographic devices, and their handlers, then a second time in order to approach Commander Tosto, a close acquaintance of hers.

"Hello, Giovanni!"

Seeing her, the huge man raised his cup of cappuccino in her direction and smiled broadly.

"Commissario!" he exclaimed in his inimitable Paler-
mitan accent. "I'm delighted to see you."

"It's always a pleasure to work with you," stammered
Simona, "but I'm not sure I can say I'm happy to see you
this time. What is this madhouse? Who is that guy?"

About ten yards behind the official, two men in
balaclavas were coming down the steps of an old building. Between them was a man much smaller in height and
build, who was hiding his face in his jacket.

Commander Tosto lowered his gaze.

"That's the porter. He's the only person who sleeps
here. We're taking him in for interrogation."

"But what is this building?"

"The seat of the Alpine Valley Beekeepers' Defense
League. We surprised the members of the group in their
homes and conducted a thorough search . . ."

"Have you found anything yet?"

Tosto looked even more uncomfortable than before.

"Commissario, I don't know if I can . . ."

"Of course. I hope the operation is a success."

Simona turned around, scanning the crowd for
Evangelisti. She saw him in the middle of an animated
throng of reporters. He saw her too. He gestured with his
hand for her to come. One of the reporters who was holding a microphone up to the magistrate turned around to

see who the gesture was directed at. It was Ciuffani. He started walking toward her.

The commissario took off in the other direction. As she made her way to the edge of the piazza she was practically running. She almost collided with a carabiniere, who was standing with his arms crossed in front of a hotel just beyond the general commotion. Looking up, she cried out:

"Calabonda!"

"Commissario, good morning," he said.

"But you're not . . ."

"No, I'm not participating in this operation. They just asked me to put my men and my workspace at the disposal of the investigators from NOCS and the General Investigations and Operations Unit. I'm only here as a spectator."

Seeing the noncommissioned officer's crestfallen expression, Simona almost felt like giving him some words of encouragement. But then she thought it might upset him, so she contented herself to nod to show that she had registered the information. Then she gestured to indicate that she would be on her way.

"Commissario," said Calabonda. "I have something to tell you."

"I'm listening."

The carabiniere cleared his throat.

"What I mean is . . . I'd like to meet somewhere else. Do you know the Chapel of San Gregorio?"

"Yes, I visited it with Marco."

"Right before you get there, on the right, there's a path through the fir trees. Take it, walk fifty yards, and wait for me."

He looked at his watch.

"A half hour from now."

Simona stared at the mustachioed face. The dark glasses made it impossible to look into his eyes. Either this guy had also fallen prey to the mental illness of the valleys, which may or may not have been caused by amped-up bee pheromones, or something very serious was going on.

"All right," she said.

*   *   *

A half hour later, Calabonda stepped out of his car and signaled to her to get out of hers.

Leaning against a larch tree ten or so feet from the beaten dirt road, he told her about the discovery of the whiskey bottle, and how they had traced it to Ciuffani. Then he told her about the interrogation at the hotel, which the reporter had interrupted to make a phone call. Afterward, Ciuffani had returned with a triumphant air.

"And that's when he said that he was sorry," continued Calabonda, "but he would have to bring the interview to a close, and that moreover I would soon receive a phone call to that effect. And with that, he turned on me and left."

Seeing as he paused, Simona asked, "And what did you do?"

"What do you think I did? I watched him leave . . . I didn't want . . . I didn't want to run the risk . . ."

Of pulling a Cacabonda, Simona finished in her head.

". . . of arresting a television reporter on my own initiative," the maresciallo continued. "But I took out my phone to call Evangelisti and tell him what had just happened. I thought he could interrogate Ciuffani personally. Except that my phone rang before I could dial the number—"

"Let me guess. It was your superior, a commander, or a captain . . ."

"It was the general commander himself! From the Turin office. He said just two words to me . . ."

"'Drop it.' Right?"

Calabonda removed his dark glasses to see her better. "Just like that. That's it exactly. He prohibited me from consulting with Evangelisti. How did you know?"

"You haven't guessed what's behind all of this?"

"The Services?"

"Well, yes. You know, I'm a habitué. They butt in whenever we're working on delicate cases having to do with the Mafia or terrorism. Think back to the time one of your colleagues was about to arrest Provenzano, well before they decided to do it themselves. Provenzano used to be responsible for maintaining the *pax mafiosa* negotiated by the State—which was made possible precisely because of the Services' involvement as an intermediary. Your colleague received the same phone call from one of his superiors."

The maresciallo's pride seemed to have disappeared completely. He looked so deflated that Simona felt something not unlike pity.

"You shouldn't let it get you down," she said. "They've inadvertently given us an essential piece of information on the case: when the Services intervene, it means that it goes all the way up to the top."

Calabonda seemed somewhat consoled by this affirmation.

"And what should I do?" he asked. "What will I do now?"

"You will obey orders. It's your military duty, isn't it?"

And seeing his unhappy expression, she added:

"I on the other hand am not a member of the military. I promise you that if there are developments, I will keep you informed," she made clear. She went to pat him on the shoulder, but she stopped herself.

Just as she was getting ready to leave, she changed her mind. "By the way, does anyone know why Bertolazzi was at Minoncelli's house?"

"Based on what we learned from Bertolazzi's cell phone, it seems he received a phone call after Minoncelli left home. The call came from Minoncelli's residence, but at that time Minoncelli was at the Claudiana bookstore in Torre Pellice. We have the Gnone brothers' testimonies to that effect: he was talking with them about organizing a debate, before going to occupy Bertolazzi's villa. Someone called Bertolazzi from Minoncelli's house and probably convinced the engineer to go there and kill him. Who? What did he say to convince him? And why did the person who made the call kill Bertolazzi? I have a lot of work to do to find the answers . . . for as long as the investigation is mine to conduct . . ."

There was an exchange of doubtful looks. Then Simona asked, "And as to the fact of my gun being stolen, have you made any progress?"

"No one noticed any intruders that morning. The maids were all in the halls the entire time, while you were having breakfast and out for a walk. It's very unlikely that someone would have been able to get into your room without being seen. I believe the thief entered the room at night while the two of you were sleeping."

"Someone very skilled then, and well equipped, because I didn't notice any signs of destructive entry. This part of your investigation is of particular interest to me, as I'm sure you can imagine. I'll have to explain what happened to my superiors. Allowing your weapon to be stolen is already a very serious thing, but when that weapon is then used to commit murder . . . I may have to face a disciplinary hearing. For the moment no one has called me—not from the DNA, not from the central direction of the police—but it won't be long now . . ."

Calabonda threw his arms open in a show of displeasure.

"It's not your fault . . . You haven't committed any sort of indiscretion."*Holy crap*, thought Simona. *Am I actually*

*seeking consolation from this sorry excuse for a country carabi-
niere . . . ?*

"I hope that my superiors see it the same way you
do," said Simona. "And that they let you investigate these
crimes as thoroughly as necessary."

And it was with these hopes, and the feeling that she
had participated in a rather whiny exchange between two
losers, that Simona parted ways with the maresciallo.

*   *   *

One hour later, settled into her hotel room bed, on her
lap a tray full of biscotti, croissants, coffee, jellies, various
types of honey, orange juice, and a piece of blueberry cake,
she watched Evangelisti's televised press conference. To his
right sat the head of DIGOS (the *Divisione Investigazioni
Generali e Operazioni Speciali,* or General Investigations
and Special Operations Division) headquarters in Turin,
to his left the representative of the district attorney's office
in that same city, with various police directors standing
behind him. At the end of the table, Simona spotted the
testy whiskers of Calabonda.

On the table in front of them was an impressive display of rifles, aerosol can bombs, stacks of pamphlets and
papers, in addition to numerous knives and other non-
firearm weapons. The camera zoomed in on them and
Simona recognized several uncapping knives. The day
before she had seen Minoncelli maneuver one of these
same tools to extract the honey from his beehives.

A school classroom had been taken over for the press conference. The reporters were seated at the students' desks and the words "Operation Edelweiss" had been written in chalk on the blackboard behind the officials.

"Weapons, materials, and documents were found at the homes of members of the Alpine Valley Beekeepers' Defense League," Evangelisti said, "all of which are about to be analyzed."

Evangelisti spoke in a tone that Simona had never heard him use before. The good-natured irony, which until then had seemed to be his trademark, had completely disappeared. He was so focused and solemn that a second went by before a reporter asked him:

"Have you found evidence of the League's involvement in the failed attack on the Sacropiano research center in Pinerolo?"

Without any change in his focused expression, Evangelisti answered, "Our attention was drawn to a brief pamphlet entitled 'The Worker Bee Revolution,' of which we found numerous copies at the homes of the arrestees. The fact that the title corresponds to the words painted on the wall at the Sacropiano research center and scrawled on several pieces of paper found at the sites of the two murders is certainly no coincidence. It seems the pamphlet had circulated in secret for several weeks. What we're dealing with is a text that questions the most fundamental aspects of democratic society and invites readers to 'desert' various institutions.

The investigators are in the process of determining whether the term 'desert' could be code for 'sabotage.'"

Simona guffawed, dunking a spoon in a jar of rosemary honey.

"Aside from these sheets of paper and the pamphlet, do you have anything else to implicate the League in the murders of Bertolazzi and Danela, who was a well-known enemy of Minoncelli?"

Evangelisti exchanged a few hushed words with the head of DIGOS before turning to face the cameras again.

"At this point in the investigation, we prefer to refrain from providing further information . . ."

"But do you have proof that this pamphlet was produced by the League or by one of its members?" inquired a representative of the print media.

Evangelisti shook his head.

"For the moment, we cannot provide further information."

One man stood up from his desk abruptly, almost knocking it over. Simona recognized Giuseppe Felice. His voice, at first uncertain, slowly became more confident as he formulated his question. "Is it true that Minoncelli was not arrested because you did not find him at his residence, or at the apiary?"

"Yes, that's true," Evangelisti answered. "But his arrest will come shortly. If he's listening, I encourage him to go to the nearest carabinieri headquarters. It is in his best interest. We urgently need him to clarify the role played by each member of the League. I am not accusing the Defense League in its entirety, but it is possible that a secret faction has developed within the organization. We are simply interested in separating the good eggs from the bad, the right of democratic protest from terrorism. That is in the common interest. Ladies, gentlemen, this concludes the press conference," he finished, standing up.

Simona turned off the television and, with a grim expression on her face, began to make every last edible thing on the tray disappear between her full lips. When she had finished, she let out a faint burp, got out of the bed, set the tray down on the ground, and went to the bathroom to throw up. *This makes me feel young*, she thought, her hands clutching the rim of the toilet bowl, her face covered in cold sweat. Between the ages of twenty and thirty-five she had been thin thanks to what could be called "functional anorexia." Then she decided that she could live without attracting men, and within a few months she had gained several pounds and met Marco. They had seduced each other reciprocally, and in spite of their many amorous escapades, the relationship had stuck.

She was splashing some water on her face in front of the bathroom mirror when the phone rang. She took her time drying off, then answered.

"Ah, Simona!" exclaimed the interlocutor, relieved.

It was Antonio Bianchi, prosecutor for the National Antimafia Administration, to which the commissario reported directly.

"Good morning, Prosecutor. Are you calling to reprimand me?"

"Good morning, Commissario," Bianchi said, in a warmer tone than the one she had expected. "I'm calling to tell you to be careful. As far as the theft of your gun is concerned—"

"I'm prepared to make a statement to the disciplinary committee," Simona cut in, running a hand through her hair.

It was in need of a good brushing.

"We're not at that point. You will explain yourself to your superiors, and if they don't find you guilty of neglect, it will end there. In the end, they were the ones who proposed that you carry it with you during vacations . . . No, I'm calling to ask you to avoid getting yourself mixed up in the murder and failed attack case in the valley altogether. I've discussed it with the Turin district attorney's office and we decided that your presence in the region is no longer necessary. Of course, I know you like to foster collaboration between organizations, and I know in the future you will want to be where you are needed. However, I can't deny that your presence right now is creating a somewhat awkward situation for the investigators. You needlessly attract the attention of certain media outlets that are hostile to our interests . . ."

"You want me to get off their asses, pronto, is that it?"

Bianchi chuckled.

"I wouldn't express it in quite those terms, but that is the substance of the message."

"All right, but I'll have to wait for my darling husband, who is on his way back from Salina. Marco was getting bored without me." (*And he didn't want to leave me alone with the handsome Minoncelli*, she added mentally, smiling.) "Let's say that we'll leave tomorrow morning at the latest."

There was a brief silence, then:

"Understood. Tomorrow morning. At the latest," he repeated. "Spend the rest of your vacation somewhere relaxing and come back fully refreshed, Simona. We need you here."

"Thank you, Signor Prosecutor. You can count on me."

As she hung up, Simona thought, *That's what I call a clear message. If you can't stop being a pest, there's no guarantee you'll be able to continue with your antimafia investigations.*

After she'd taken a long shower, during which she massaged herself with a Chinese anticellulite brush and washed her hair with a nourishing avocado shampoo, she dried off using a frizz-control hairdryer, rubbed various lotions on her body, hands, and face, and chose a charming floral button-up shirt and a pair of slimming black pants that flattered her still slender waist. Then she placed her solid bottom, which still gave Marco heart palpitations and had stirred the desires of numerous colleagues, on a backless chair in front of the large desk belonging to the hotel. She opened her computer and checked her email.

Giuseppe Felice had sent her the photos taken at the murder sites right before the departure of the Forensics team.

She studied the photo that had grabbed her attention.

In the place of several objects that the officials had packaged and taken away, they had drawn their exact positions in chalk and placed small, numbered signs to indicate the identities of the missing objects.

She thought for a long time, her eyes fixed on the photo; then a noise made her turn. Someone had stuck something under her door. She jumped up and threw the door open.

The hallway was deserted; the light above the elevator at the end of the hall flashed. Simona shrugged. There was no way of knowing whether the person who slid the thing under her door had taken the elevator or the stairs, going up or going down. The hotel was full of places to hide. Any attempt at pursuing them would be pointless.

She returned to her room. The object that they had slid under the door was a thin, bound pamphlet entitled "The Worker Bee Revolution." There was no author. The commissario picked it up, then took her cell phone from the nightstand, removed the battery, stuffed everything in her purse, and left. She went down into the hotel parking garage and stationed herself in the shadows near her car, patiently waiting for someone to decide to come out. Sitting on an old toolbox behind a column, she reflected: on her life, on her relationship with the law enforcement organization for which she had worked for nearly thirty years, on her relationship with Marco. On everything except for the case of the murderers in the valley. Finally, a couple of arguing forty-year-olds turned up in the parking garage and, still arguing, got into a high-end convertible. As soon as the metal door began to close behind the vehicle, Simona made her exit.

She squinted in the sunlight, not noticing anything in particular. She walked quickly along the street where the hotel was and turned onto the first road that crossed it. A half hour later, from a phone booth near San Giorgio al Monte's old station (two tourist trains per day), she called Giuseppe Felice.

"Good morning, Giuseppe, this is Simona Tavianello. I need a little information . . . No, wait, listen, it's urgent. All right, call Evangelisti. Really insist on speaking with him personally. Explain that it's very important and very urgent. Whatever you do, do not tell him you're calling on my behalf. Don't mention my name. Simply ask him whether Item Number 78C turned up any interesting results, or whether it happened to go missing, by chance. Yes . . . got it? I'll call you back in a half hour."

She hung up and looked around her. All in all, she had to admit that walking a mile in a fugitive's shoes wasn't a bad workout. But she decided that her little game had gone on long enough, and took off heading west, toward the nameless café where she had met Felice and Minoncelli.

When she walked in twenty minutes later, she was not surprised to find the reporter at his usual table. When he saw her, he jumped. It was getting to be a habit.

"But shouldn't you have—"

"Called you again? Well, the truth is that I prefer to talk face to face. So, how did Evangelisti respond?"

The redheaded little scarecrow grinned wider than she had ever seen him grin.

"It wasn't easy getting through to him directly, but I finally managed it. As usual, he used the same annoyed yet courteous tone with me that he uses with everyone—the tone you use on the phone when you're trying to get rid of someone who's bothering you—until he heard my question. He went totally quiet. Then he said, 'What number?' And I repeated it for him: 'Item Number 78C.' Then he coughed and said, 'I'll call you back'—very low, almost in a whisper. And there you have it. I'm still waiting for his call."

Simona looked up in the direction of the café owner, but right then Felice's cell phone rang. He glanced at the display and said, "Ah, no, it's not him. It's my editorial director. Dottore Alberto Signorelli."

He answered.

"Good morning, Dottore. Yes, that's right . . . have you called him? Ah, in that case I should . . . Oh really? What are we dealing with exactly? I don't know, this is strictly based on a tip I received, I'm not sure I should reveal my source . . ."

Simona, who was staring at him, nodded vigorously.

"Oh, all right, she says I can tell you. It's Commissario Tavianello . . . Yes, yes, she's sitting across from me. All right . . ."

The reporter held out the phone to the policewoman.

"He wants to talk to you."

With her face screwed up into a puzzled expression, Simona brought the object to her ear.

"Good morning, Commissario," said a deep voice.

"Good morning, Dottore. You wanted to speak with me?"

"Yes, but not over the phone. In person, if you don't mind."

"Yes, certainly. When?"

"Immediately. If you don't mind."

"But how—"

"I just parked my car across the street from the café. I'll wait for you."

Simona returned the device to the reporter, his eyes open wide, and walked out of the café. On the other side of the road, flanked by two poplars, was a luxury sports sedan with tinted windows. As soon as the commissario had crossed the street, the left rear door opened.

Leaning over, she saw a corpulent man in a corduroy suit. In his bloated features she could detect a resemblance to those of Francesco Signorelli, the executive director of the Sacropiano research center in Pinerolo. He patted the seat next to him with a fat-fingered hand.

"Please," he said. "We'll be better off chatting here than in that hole-in-the-wall so beloved by my employee."

Simona settled into the ample leather seat and the automatic door closed behind her silently. A faint scent of lavender reigned in the cockpit. All she could see of the driver was his broad back and the folds in the back of his neck below the traditional visored cap.

"Pleased to make your acquaintance," Signorelli said as he gave her his giant hand for a shake. "We were on our way to my office when I received a phone call from Evangelisti. That magistrate seems to think that because I am the principal heir to our family's fortune, my work at *Il Quotidiano delle Valli* must just be something I do to pass the time. Perhaps he also thinks that I'm prepared to do anything and everything to help that idiot brother of mine out of a sense of family solidarity. You know, he actually called me to ask that I intimate to Felice to drop this whole thing about Item Number 78C. He's out of luck. Understand that I belong to a disappearing species in Italy: I'm for a journalism uninfluenced by the powers that be."

He paused, giving the narrator—who relies on critics' benevolence with regard to his work—time to point out that these statements are the dottore's own, and he alone is responsible for them. Then Alberto Signorelli added:

"On top of that, Francesco is a fucking moron. And I don't know what he's up to at his research center, but I smell a rat. So, what is this Item Number 78C?"

"A red marker. Now, the piece of paper with the words 'The Worker Bee Revolution' on it, found near Bertolazzi's body, was written in red marker. It would be interesting to know whether any fingerprints or DNA were found on this marker. Did Evangelisti tell you anything about this piece of evidence?"

Alberto Signorelli slapped his thigh with a triumphant expression.

"Ah, well yes, he told me that the item unfortunately disappeared from the shelves of the court's records office, and he emphasized that we mustn't press the point; they would certainly get it back, but a pointless little scandal could delay Operation Edelweiss, which was aimed at preemptively eliminating any threat from the ecoterrorists, who could still consider my brother's research center a target. He also told me how he was in favor of the concept of 'preventive detection,' a crime prevention method that consists of individuating the dangers posed by certain organizations, even before they actually become dangerous, and intervening based not on what people have done but on what they are likely to do. I told him in that case I should be arrested immediately, because I often feel like strangling my wife."

"Did he laugh?"

"He laughed. The idiot thought I was joking!" boomed the director of the *Quotidiano delle Valli*, eyeballing his conversation partner.

When Simona didn't bat an eyelash, he added:

"He also told me in confidence that they brought you in on the investigation in order to keep an eye on you."

Simona smiled.

"You know, I had my suspicions."

Again, the esteemed director slapped himself squarely on the thigh.

"I like you, Commissario! I've always sworn by full-figured women."

Simona chose not to reflect on this compliment.

"Is that why you wanted to speak with me? To warn me?"

"To warn you and tell you that I won't pass on a big story to protect my idiot brother. You have the *Quotidiano delle Valli*'s support."

Simona pushed back a white wisp of hair that was covering her eye.

"I am sorry to disappoint you, Signor Signorelli, but my involvement in this case will be limited to my having pointed out the importance of a piece of evidence to your reporter. As for the rest, I have faith in his capabilities and in his willingness to fight . . ."

"Capable and willing to fight—he'd better be, that asshole, if he wants to eat! But you're right, there's more to him than meets the eye. Maybe I've underestimated him. At any rate, this whole Operation Edelweiss thing is ridiculous. Those weapons . . . everyone in the valley is laughing about them. Discovering hunting rifles at the homes of the valley's inhabitants is an absolute joke! Everyone hunts here, including beekeepers

. . . That doesn't change the fact that those men died. If I understand correctly, you don't intend to continue investigating?"

"It's not my place. Tomorrow morning I'm leaving for a vacation under more peaceful skies, accompanied by my husband."

"Shame . . ." said Signorelli, sizing her up with a movement of his large nose that was reminiscent of a boar in search of strong, appetizing odors. "Shall we take you back to your hotel?"

Simona could feel the strain from the walk in her legs and gladly accepted.

*　*　*

When she was back in her room, she felt a tremendous sleepiness weighing her down, and as soon as she lay down on the bed, she fell asleep.

When she woke up, it was four in the afternoon. She had slept five hours straight. She had an incredible ability to take refuge in sleep and linger there, at any hour of the day, when the world around her seemed dark and hostile. A shame that she didn't have the same gift as a commissario friend of hers who solved enigmas in his sleep.

She called to order a snack of prosciutto and local cheese, accompanied by an excellent Piedmontese beer. While she was eating she glanced at the dark screen of her television and decided to leave it that way.

Later, after slaloming through the lobby to avoid the group of reporters, she set herself up on a chaise lounge at the far end of the hotel garden, underneath a bougainvillea buzzing with insects. She immersed herself in "The Worker Bee Revolution."

The text began as follows:

> The specialists who have written on colony collapse disorder point out that the sudden disappearance of the worker bees is much worthier of attention when dead bees aren't found in the area surrounding the beehive. It can be broadly deduced that they went elsewhere to die. And what if they did not? What if, rather than going off to die, they regrouped and went to live somewhere else, away from that place of exploitation and pollution, where they were exposed to the disease that is the hive? And what if the disappearance of the bees were actually mass desertion? What if the bees we believe to be dead were living elsewhere, like the Maroons who once fled the plantations where they were reduced to slavery, in Haiti or in the other Caribbean islands? What if the bees have gone into hiding?

"That's good reading you have there," said a voice that Simona recognized immediately.

Minoncelli crouched down, bending his large frame so that his blue eyes could meet with those of Simona.

"Oh good, it's you!" exclaimed Simona. "Do you know that they're looking for you?"

"Yes, I know. I plan on going to the court tonight with my lawyer. This entire operation is monstrous, as well you know."

Simona inspected that hunk of a man and his undying smile.

"I don't know. I'm not going to criticize my colleagues. There was, after all, an attempted attack . . . and there have been several deaths . . ."

"As far as the attempted attack is concerned, you must excuse me for having my doubts. It serves the purpose of supporting the ecoterrorism theory and putting an end to the League's protests against Sacropiano's experiments in the valley once and for all. We don't know exactly what kind of shady dealings they're running in their laboratory, and thanks to this whole mess, maybe we never will. It wouldn't be the first time a fake terrorist plot was used to stamp out dissent . . ."

"That's what we call a conspiracy theory."

"You're not going to tell me that conspiracies don't exist in Italy?"

Simona looked down to protect herself from the influence of that truly intense gaze.

"Who wrote this?" she asked, indicating the pamphlet with a quick movement of her chin.

"I don't know anything about it. We received a pack of them at our headquarters. We thought it was interesting, though it is fairly unhinged . . . As you can see, there aren't any names on the front."

As he said this, he pulled the cover of the pamphlet, which was still in Simona's hands, back into place.

It was in this position, him crouching near her, their hands very close together and holding the same book, that Marco Tavianello surprised them.

"Am I interrupting something?"

CHAPTER 8

*A*s awkward as that moment was, Simona was saved
from yet another inconvenient misapprehension, taunting,
a man-on-man boxing match, and other trials that have
assailed the majority of living creatures since the dawn of
sexual reproduction, by her spontaneous reaction: When
she saw her husband standing there, fuming, she burst out
laughing. Then she threw herself into his arms.

"Marco! I'm so happy to see you!" she cried.

"I'm not interrupting?"

"Don't talk nonsense, you Neapolitan macho! This is
Giovanni Minoncelli."

The two men shook hands.

"Well, finally!" exclaimed Marco. "The last time we
tried to meet you, we found a dead body at your house. But
aren't they looking for you? Don't tell me that my wife has
let herself enter into an illicit friendship with a fugitive?"

"I'm going to present myself at the courthouse with my lawyer shortly, but first I wanted to say a few words to your wife . . . and to you, if you'd like to listen."

The two men sat down on two metal chairs next to Simona, who had settled back into her lounger. Minoncelli repeated what he had just said to the commissario, and Marco, considering the possibility that Operation Edelweiss served primarily to protect Sacropiano's experiments, refrained from hinting at conspiracy theories, as his wife had done, and said simply:

"It's not impossible." But he added, "Do you have an alibi for the night of the attack?"

Minoncelli shook his head.

"No. Evangelisti let me go, and I went home without meeting anyone."

Marco shook his head before calmly offering his take on the situation.

"In that case, my wife will have to arrest you."

The beekeeper jumped up from his seat.

"What are you talking about?"

"What are you saying?" asked Simona, sitting up in turn.

Marco stayed in his chair but reached out his hands, his palms facing forward.

"Calm yourselves. Think about it for a second. If you want us to help you, Minoncelli, we have to operate within the strictest confines of the law; that way Evangelisti and the rest—everyone behind him, the Services, and the other authorities—can only praise us for intervening. If we arrest the main suspect for the attempted attacks, I don't see how they could keep us from sticking around here and butting in a little while longer . . ."

Simona had kept her eyes on him from the moment he began his response.

"What's gotten into you?" she grumbled. "I'd like an explanation. I thought you'd come back to take me to Salina . . . because, well, I don't know . . ."

She went silent, though she couldn't resist shooting a sideways glance at the handsome beekeeper.

"Well," cautioned Marco, "if you don't know, it'd be better not to discuss it. It just so happens that I made a few phone calls on my way back, and I realized this case was getting to be of interest to many of us, including those who, like you and I, are rather sick of the Services' dirty little games."

Ah, thought Simona, *he called his brothers in the Freemasons. That was the only thing missing from this affair.* But she stayed quiet.

"Listen to me," he said to Minoncelli. "You can trust me. You have more powerful allies than you even know. Not everyone in the upper echelons of the government agrees with what's happening at Sacropiano's laboratories. Do you have a vague idea of what they're up to?"

Minoncelli shook his head.

"Bertolazzi didn't want to tell me. Yes," he said in response to Marco's thunderstruck expression, "we were in touch. He didn't make it known officially, in the interest of keeping his job. But after talking with us and reading up on the bee problem, which wasn't his area of expertise, he ending up seeing things our way. He was even worried toward the end; he would say to me, 'You don't know what they're doing,' referring to Sacropiano's research. He wouldn't say any more than that because he said it was too dangerous, but he encouraged me to continue fighting his company. When we occupied his villa, he and I had arranged it beforehand in secret—no one else in the League knew. He told me that we'd find some documents in his desk that would show what they were plotting at the Sacropiano laboratories. But because things went the way they did, I didn't have time to go through the desk in question. They told me he was dead, the carabinieri came for me, and the occupation was cut short. I'm guessing that Sacropiano has gotten hold of the documents by now."

"All right," Marco said firmly, "we'll take care of it. One way or another, we will find a way to make this corporation tell us what it's up to. Do you agree to let Simona arrest you?"

Minoncelli flashed his broad, irresistible smile.

"Well!" he said, turning toward the commissario, "I've never been handcuffed by a beautiful woman before. I'd love to try it!"

"I'm sorry to disappoint you," the commissario shot back in the same tone. "I don't bring handcuffs on vacation."

Then she stopped smiling. Out of the corner of her eye, she saw Marco's face turning purple. He inhaled deeply, unclenched his fists, and said, "Let's go. Simona, you'll have to call Calabonda to tell him that we're bringing Minoncelli to him."

The maresciallo answered on the second ring, listened to what the commissario had to tell him, and blurted out, "I'm busy. But I'll send a car to get him. It'll be there in ten minutes."

The beekeeper's journey across the park and over to the police car in the company of Signor and Signora Tavianello did not go unobserved. There were shouts and mad dashes from the cameramen and photographers who had abandoned their equipment to enjoy the pool for a minute. Ciuffani ended up in a shrub in an attempt to find a shortcut that would allow him to beat his colleagues. Marco unloaded some of his nervous energy by dealing a few blows to people's stomachs with his elbows. Right before he was handcuffed by a carabiniere and loaded into the car with a hand guiding his head, Minoncelli shot Simona a look in which she perceived, for the first time, fear and dismay.

"I hope I can trust you," he said.

As the car departed and they fought off the microphones, Marco mumbled to his wife, "All right, now that we've gotten rid of that asshole, can we finally go on our vacation?"

Simona stared at her husband. He didn't seem to be joking. She answered her cell phone, which was ringing. It was Calabonda.

"It seems you are still indispensable," the carabiniere said to her. "I'm at the hospital. I have permission to speak with Mehmet Berisha, but he says that he will only speak in your presence. He only trusts you, because you saved his life. And also because, in his words, 'you at least, when he speaks, understand it.'"

"All right, I'm coming," Simona said. Then she met her husband's gaze, cleared her throat, and stammered, "That is . . . hmm, yes, perhaps . . . oh, very well, fine." As she ended the call, she locked eyes with Marco. "I'm coming. See you soon," she finished. "Will you come with me?" she asked Marco.

He shook his head.

"I came here to get you, not to conduct an unauthorized investigation. Let me remind you that I'm retired. I'm leaving tomorrow. And this time, if you don't come with me, I'll spend my vacation alone."

And he turned away.

* * *

The air conditioning in the crowded hospital room at Ospedale Civile Edoardo Agnelli was out of order, but Mehmet Berisha, in spite of the heavy sheet and the fact that his leg was in a cast and in traction, seemed to be the only one unfazed by the heat. Evangelisti, sitting on an adjustable chair upholstered in gray plastic, kept unsticking his sweat-soaked back from the backrest and fanning himself with a sheet of paper that had wilted from the temperature. Calabonda, leaning against the bathroom door, had removed his cap and was looking inside it with a gloomy expression. The interpreter, sitting on a stool by Mehmet's bedside, was dripping with sweat, as was the carabiniere responsible for taking down the deposition, who had set up a laptop and printer on a rolling table with an adjustable top.

"Good morning, miss," Mehmet said to Simona in English as she settled against the post from which his leg was suspended at the foot of the bed.

"Good morning, Signor Berisha," she answered. "We're ready."

The shepherd nodded and started talking. Speaking in a monotone, he explained that he had been in a romantic relationship with Maurizio Bertolazzi, the engineer, for two months, and that he suspected he was cheating on him with Giovanni Minoncelli.

"How did you come to have these suspicions?" asked Calabonda.

The interpreter translated and Mehmet Berisha shrugged. He said something that included the word "gay." The interpreter, an abundantly mustachioed carabiniere from an Albanian community in Aspromonte, Calabria, seemed surprised. He questioned him, and Berisha answered.

"What is he saying?" inquired Evangelisti.

"He says he knows Minoncelli is gay," responded the mustachioed man, "because he and Bertolazzi ran into him in a gay bar in Turin."

Simona ran a hand over her head and got mad at herself for the feeling of disappointment that suddenly washed over her. How were Minoncelli's habits any of her business?

"The deposition will continue," added Evangelisti, "and you," he said turning to face the carabiniere-interpreter, "limit yourself to translating. Don't intervene in his statement."

Berisha explained that he had noticed after the town hall meeting that Minoncelli and Bertolazzi were always finding secluded spots to chat, and that Bertolazzi would have a smitten look on his face. He knew that look well, he did . . . And then, three days earlier, Bertolazzi had called him to cancel a date; they were supposed to meet at his villa in Torre Pellice and spend the night there. Berisha went to his lover's house anyway. The lights were out in the windows and he waited all night for the engineer to return. In the morning he decided to go to Minoncelli's house. When he got there someone whose face he didn't see was driving away from the beekeeper's property. It wasn't Minoncelli's car, but Berisha thought maybe he had gotten a new one. At any rate, the shepherd walked toward the house, tried the doorknob, and seeing as it wasn't locked, went in. He went to check out the bedroom; the sheets were rumpled and he thought he picked up on the smell of sex. As an incredible anger built up inside him, he grabbed the telephone and hit the redial button. It was Bertolazzi's cell phone number.

His dark gaze was trained on Simona. The shepherd spoke his own language, the Calabrian carabiniere translated, his colleague tapped away at the computer keyboard, and it kept getting hotter.

"Could we open it, perhaps?" asked the commissario, pointing to the window.

The maresciallo nodded. He went to turn the handle and pulled, almost falling on the bed. A bit of cool air entered the room.

"Continue," Evangelisti ordered, after an irritated cluck of the tongue.

Bertolazzi picked up on the first ring. When he heard Berisha's voice, the engineer's tone grew very concerned. The shepherd suggested they meet right away; he wanted an explanation. At first Bertolazzi said he needed to go to Turin for an important meeting, but when the Albanian threatened to turn Minoncelli's house upside down, he said he would be there in twenty minutes. While he was waiting Berisha rummaged around and found a gun in the beekeeper's desk drawer.

"Wait," interrupted Evangelisti, "what gun? Can you describe it?"

The shepherd frowned, and, with the aid of some hand movements and a great deal of precision in his use of the terminology (he had spent ten years in the Albanian army), he described the Beretta 92 SBM firearm— a weapon used by women and officials due to its small size and the fact that it could be easily concealed. It was without a doubt the same model as Simona's stolen weapon.

Calabonda leaned over to the commissario and said to her in a hushed voice, "In effect, your fingerprints are on the weapon."

The Albanian finished his story: subsequently, when Bertolazzi returned, they had argued violently. The engineer told him he didn't want to see him anymore, and the shepherd had shot him with the Beretta.

Silence fell. Large, round tears rolled down the shepherd's unshaven cheeks. Someone coughed; someone shifted in a chair; Evangelisti fanned himself furiously without saying a word.

Finally, the maresciallo asked, "And the sheet of paper with the words 'The Worker Bee Revolution' written on it, where did you get the idea to place it on the body?"

Berisha looked surprised when he heard the translation. He shook his head and said a few monosyllabic words.

"He doesn't know what you're talking about," the carabiniere said.

"He didn't write 'The Worker Bee Revolution' in red marker on a sheet of paper left on or near the body?" Calabonda persisted.

He denied it again. Simona asked Calabonda with her eyes if she could ask a question. He nodded.

"How did you meet Bertolazzi?" she asked.

Berisha tried to sit up a little, tugging on his leg, which caused the bar that held it in traction to sway violently. He abandoned this effort and began to speak in a halting voice. A ridge high above his cabin, some charcoal-colored rocks emerging from a stony trail, the figure of the engineer appearing suddenly while the shepherd is lying in wait for a mountain goat he has been tracking for a couple of hours. It was there they saw each other for the first time. Bertolazzi had told him he loved walking in the mountains; he had been hiking farther down, near the lake, when he noticed, in amazement, what he thought was a swarm of bees. He had followed them up there, but the swarm had disappeared. After that they made their way down to the shepherd's hovel and spent their first night together.

After Bertolazzi's death, he had wanted to return to the place where they'd met, up near those black rocks that jutted out from the stony trail. But as he was making the climb he'd heard a blast from a nearby ridge and he'd caught a bullet in the knee, perhaps from an off-target hunter, or who knows what. Regardless, he regretted just one thing now: that whoever shot that bullet hadn't gotten him right in the head.

With these last words, the Albanian's mouth remained open a moment. He kept his gaze fixed on Simona. Then, suddenly, a long moan emerged from his full, painfully chapped lips.

"Get the doctor," said Evangelisti. "The wound must be causing him a lot of pain."

The interpreter rushed out of the room. Simona shrugged.

"I don't think it's the leg that's hurting him. And I think it would be better to leave him in peace."

"I agree," said Calabonda. "But we still need him to sign the deposition."

The commissario looked away from the Albanian's gaze. "I'll wait for you in the hallway."

When she went to push the door open she caught a glimpse of something moving sideways. She stuck her head out and saw a figure hurrying toward the elevator. She could run very fast for a woman of her size, and she found herself face to face with the fugitive just as the elevator doors were closing.

"It's you, you piece of shit!" she shouted.

They weren't alone. Two nurses were keeping a dazed old man company. He was wearing a hospital gown and sitting in a wheelchair with his arm hooked up to an IV, which one of the women distractedly held in place as she and her colleague jabbered on about the bad-tempered head nurse. When they heard Simona cry out, the nurses went silent, darting glances at her with a mixture of curiosity and concern.

The person Simona had addressed so indignantly, a bald man who was elegant in spite of a little extra weight around his midsection, flashed a courteous smile at the two ladies.

"My colleague has always had a penchant for flowery language," he said. "But she's a true professional."

The nurses giggled and got off on the next floor, pushing the old man as he drooled a bit on his neck. Simona stopped the elevator between two floors and planted herself in front of the control panel, using her solid body as a shield.

"When I saw that Ciuffani was on the scene, I knew the Services had to be behind it," she said, crossing her arms in front of her. "It's like they say: even paranoid people have their enemies. Was it marksmen who shot down Danela and wounded Berisha?"

The man shrugged.

"Why would we start shooting people over some bees? We have a sense of proportion, after all."

Simona stared back at him and shrugged in turn.

"To tell the truth, I believe you. But what about my gun being stolen?"

The man burst out laughing.

"Yes, well, that little trick *was* suited to the circumstances. Some activists start harassing a laboratory after we've been asked to protect it, and then wouldn't you know it, along comes Commissario Tavianello, the same dreaded ballbuster who's thrown a wrench in our operations more times than I care to count. You have to admit it was quite a feat, our getting into your room while you were sleeping; and may I just say, your chief of police snores like a hippopotamus, and so do you. Anyway, it was a nice bit of ingenuity on our part: on top of breaking into your suitcase without your realizing it the next day—yes, these are things you must be able to do in our line of work—we steal your firearm, landing both you and Minoncelli in deep shit. All we have to do from there is phone the carabinieri and report that the beekeeper has a stolen weapon in his possession, and we take out two birds with one stone."

"Except that things didn't go as planned."

"Ah, no. The Albanian showed up. I just barely managed to avoid him."

"But he didn't leave . . ."

The bald man threw his arms open wide in exasperation.

"What can I tell you? I couldn't have known . . . I was just trying to keep an eye on things . . . and when he fired the gun, well, it was too late then, wasn't it?"

"That didn't keep you from going back to put that sheet of paper on Bertolazzi's body that said 'The Worker Bee Revolution.'"

"Nice instincts, wouldn't you say?" the man snorted. "We were aware of the existence of a pamphlet that was circulating among the beekeepers, though we hadn't managed to determine the author . . . Well, it's true I misplaced the marker. I thought I'd stuck it in my pocket but I must have missed. I have to admit that I had a little whiskey after the gun went off. To reflect."

"Didn't it occur to you that you'd done enough already?"

"And you, didn't it occur to you to stop meddling in matters that don't concern you? What do you think you're going to accomplish? You want to change the world, or what? Regardless, this conversation never happened."

Simona nodded.

"Understood. But just out of curiosity . . . that other sheet of paper, the one that was left on the body of Danela, the guy who destroyed the apiary . . ."

"Ah," said the man. "No, no . . . Apparently I started a trend. But would you mind starting the elevator again? It's hot as hell in here."

"All right," she said. "But you realize that a man is dead because of you? Dead by my weapon?"

"Oh, we could even say it was your fault, if we liked. You shouldn't let yourself fall into such a deep sleep when you're carrying a weapon in your suitcase. Of course, after the good screwing that Marco gave you . . . Seriously, how do you two do it? Does he take Viagra? And you, you don't have any problems with vaginal dryness . . . ?"

Simona breathed in, breathed out, pushed the button. Then as the elevator started down again, she turned to face the man.

"What did you say a minute ago? That I was a ball-buster?"

Without giving him time to respond, her foot flew up, striking the federal agent in his lower abdomen. He howled and dropped to his knees. Clutching his holy bits, he spat out:

"You dirty communist whore! You'll pay for this, you big, fat, crooked slut! We recorded all of your little play sessions. We'll put them on the Internet!"

"You poor asshole. Don't even bother. I'd love it!"

She got off on the ground floor and hurried straight for the exit. Outside, large drops of rain had started to fall.

*　　*　　*

"Did you really say that? That you'd love for them to put recordings of us screwing on the Internet?" Marco asked her a little while later.

"Well, yeah. I'm pretty proud that we still screw like maniacs after all these years. Aren't you?"

"Well, sure, but . . . What are you doing? . . . Stop it! This room is definitely bugged. They're listening to us right now . . ."

"So? Who gives a crap! Come here . . . Listen, I, hmm, see that the best part of you understands me and is showing me its approval. C'mon, come here . . ."

"Simona, you're really . . . really . . ."

Sighs. Sounds of kissing and bed springs creaking. [*Transmission interrupted.*]

*　　*　　*

"Really? You agree? We'll go back tomorrow?"

"Of course, dear, of course. This case is going to fizzle out anyway. Sooner or later Minoncelli and the others will be set free . . ."

"Ah, so that's who you're really thinking of. Your Minoncelli."

"Stop talking nonsense. Besides, he's gay!"

"Pssht! What are you talking about? Minoncelli, gay? Please, I've done my research. He's a lady-killer."

"But Berisha said that he and Bertolazzi had run into him in a gay bar in Turin."

"So what? You know it's the latest thing to knock one back with the queers!"

"Watch your mouth! So if I understand correctly, you checked up on Minoncelli because you're a big jealous idiot?"

"Not at all. It was just to get a clear picture of the situation."

"A clear picture! Listen, I'll show you a clear picture! Take a look. How do you like it?"

"Simona, you're out of control! What got you into this state? Was it getting picked up by Minoncelli?"

"So what if it was? Even if that were true, you're the one who's benefitting from it now, so what do you have to complain about?"

"Mmmmmh."

"I love shutting you up this way . . ."

[*Transmission interrupted.*]

* * *

Professor Martini ran a light hand over the pyramid of reeds arranged among two enormous bellflower bushes. Inside were the *Osmia cornuta, Osmia caerulescens, Osmia adunca, Megachile willughbiella, Eucera longicornis,* and all the rest of them. Every one of them buzzing, coming and going, transporting the professor's honey mixture, and building their nests.

"Good-bye, my dears," he said quietly.

Kneeling down to pick up his backpack, Martini felt a stabbing pain in his lower vertebrae. *After the age of fifty, if you wake up in the morning and you don't feel pain somewhere in your body, it means you're dead,* he thought as a way of consoling himself. *Fine. Besides, soon I won't have any pain anywhere,* he added straightaway. He pulled the straps of his backpack over his shoulders, pushed the green door open, and walked out into the garden. Outside, the fountain was singing. He turned to face the mountain vista. He thought he could make out, above the agate lake, far off in the distance, the sea of rocks and stones where he had an appointment.

* * *

By the time Marco emerged from the shower, Simona had finished getting dressed.

"Wow!" he exclaimed. "You look stunning! Are we going to a castle tonight?"

"Exactly, darling. While you were sleeping I got a call from Dottore Alberto Signorelli. We're invited to dine at the castle. His brother Francesco will be there as well; he's the executive director of the Sacropiano research center in Pinerolo. As will our friend Felice, the local reporter who's not as dumb as he looks."

CHAPTER 9

SOMEWHERE BETWEEN THE VILLAGES OF PINEROLO and Sestriere, just before arriving at Chisone Valley, of which it is a branch, the valley of San Giorgio al Monte becomes such a narrow ravine that the road and the railroad tracks that run alongside it have to go through a tunnel. On the other side of the stream, which barrels down into the Chisone, the Signorelli castle is perched on top of a bluish rock, sharing with countless fortified towns of the region the role of the centuries-old sentinel incapable of stopping the countless invasions.

With its machicolated battlements and small towers added on in the nineteenth century in a proto-Disneyland style, the place seemed more picturesque than luxurious. This changed when one entered the grand hall, with its paneled ceiling adorned with ornate supports in the forms of mermaids, wolves, wild boars, and carnival figures, in front of incredibly tall three-arched windows that presented a vertiginous panorama of the valley. The divans as deep as tombs, the strange flowers on the corbels, the parquet floor covered in wild animal skins and arctic fox fur, the lectern, the ebony bookcases. Royal-blue silk curtains showed a handful of silver seraphs, embroidered by the brotherhood of weavers of Cologne, flying swiftly toward the top of an ancient-looking chimney. All of the bric-a-brac amassed by some Baudelaire- and Huysmans-loving ancestor or other had proven to be extremely pleasant for enjoying an aperitif of Drappier Brut Nature "Zéro Dosage" champagne, spoonfuls of pea-sized beluga caviar, figs filled with foie gras, and dishes containing various types of game.

"None of this bullshit compares to a nice wild boar polenta washed down with a red wine from Pinerolo," Alberto said to the Tavianellos when they thanked him for the lavish hospitality. "But my wife likes it, anyway . . . And here she is."

Dressed in ultralight taffeta, willowy yet angular, her husband's junior by at least twenty-five years, the wife standing behind her consort presented a contrast like the ones frequently observed, thought Simona, in high-net-worth families. (*In other families*, she added mentally, *the good-looking pair off with the good-looking, the ugly go with the ugly, and average ones like us go with the average*.) Signora Signorelli had just entered alongside her brother-in-law, Dottore Francesco Signorelli, who had boldly chosen a plum-colored tie for the evening.

"So good to see you again, dear Commissario," he said after quickly hugging his brother. "And to make the acquaintance of your husband as well," he added as he absentmindedly shook Marco's hand. "I'm sure it's owing to your presence that the investigation into the failed attack is moving forward in leaps and bounds . . ."

When Simona raised an eyebrow, he added:

"Come on, Commissario. I admire your discretion, but I'm sure you're aware that gas cylinders like the ones used by the terrorists have been found at the homes of certain beekeepers . . ."

"Really? Gas cylinders? And they're being used as evidence?"

"Oh," said Giuseppe Felice, popping out from behind the director of the research center. "A lot of beekeepers use those cylinders. They're the cartridges for the lamps they use to visit the hives at night."

Francesco Signorelli turned around and zeroed in on the reporter, who had also made an attempt to dress up: ironed jeans, a white button-up shirt, and an apple-green jacket.

"Ah, the press!" snorted the executive. "The indispensable fourth estate! As long as they don't play to too many parties at the same time . . . but at least you're not afraid," he added, eyeing Felice's red hair, "to show your true colors!"

He laughed at his joke.

Signora Signorelli shook hands with the police officers in turn before inviting everyone to be seated at the table.

"I hope that you enjoy fusion cuisine and molecular gastronomy," she exclaimed with a sideways glance at her overweight husband. "Alberto would rather force traditional food on us for every meal, but he doesn't realize that it's no longer suited to the modern lifestyle."

As she said this, she guided them into the dining room, the floor of which had a path of inlaid marble. At the center was an enormous oak table that gave the impression of having withstood many years of banquets of the kind where guests devour entire bears and deer.

When the signora of the house had seen that everyone was seated and had had one of the servants pour them each a glass of champagne, the signore raised his glass from his place at the head of the table.

"This meal serves two purposes: to bid farewell to our friends, the Tavianellos, who are leaving our rustic valleys to continue their vacation, and to reconcile with my brother. We've had our fair share of arguments in recent years," he said, turning to face Francesco, who was staring up at him with a dumbfounded expression. "My dear brother, in token of this reconciliation I want to let you know that my newspaper will not print an article that, as Evangelisti put it, runs the risk of interfering with the investigation into the failed attack on your research center. That way we hope to put an end to the question 'What happened to Item Number 78C?' After all, it's just one small detail."

Sitting across from Felice, Simona was in an ideal spot to observe the reporter change color as his employer spoke, passing from a deathly pallor to pink and finally to a deep crimson in mere seconds. As the younger brother responded, invoking the triumph of science and reason over the obscurantism of certain extremists who would like to take us back to hoeing the land and reading by candlelight, the hostess had the servants serve the first course: an ostrich emulsion with a little scoop of caramelized algae, a berry-infused foie gras semifreddo, frozen Alaskan crab bonbons, black Iberian pork mille-feuille, and licorice-marinated white truffle. As they all discussed the cesspool that Italian politics had become, they filled their stomachs with deconstructed food items that emerged from baths of liquid nitrogen or had been whipped at some unheard-of speed. The flavors had been painstakingly isolated and then reunited using the most innovative techniques of the day, the textures undone and redone with a decidedly postmodern eye. The spices and touches of exoticism commingled to form a sort of background noise, like the languages spoken in the interpreters' booths at the United Nations, and each new dish was a surprise to behold.

If the other guests swallowed it all down with due diligence, Simona just barely nibbled at it, claiming a slight indisposition. Marco's stomach, which hadn't seen food since his departure from Salina, hesitated midway between literally shrinking from the challenge and facing it head-on. After a while, seeing as the group was admiring the plating of a particularly successful maple syrup pig's foot charlotte with lobster and pili pili Chantilly cream, their hostess asked the retired chief of police what he thought of the dinner menu, and he answered:

"This isn't a dinner . . ."

But seeing her stiffen in her chair, he hastened to add:

"It's so much more. It's a work of art . . . It's . . . an installation!"

Signora Signorelli turned red with pleasure, looked at her guests, and, with visible effort, as if Marco's compliment had given her the courage she'd been trying to summon herself, she turned to her husband to ask if he was enjoying the food he'd been putting away since the meal began without batting an eye or saying a word.

Dottore Alberto Signorelli raised his big bulging eyes to look at her and, in a voice that was utterly neutral, said, "It's very good, darling."

The signora's large, pale eyes suddenly filled with tears as she rose from her chair.

"You . . . You're only saying that to make fun of me . . ."

Alberto Signorelli lifted a reassuring hand, and as he did so, his imposing corporeal mass seemed to become somehow rounder and more compact.

"Of course not, darling . . . it's . . . it's all very good," he assured her, in a voice that evinced an attempt at enthusiasm.

The signora's delicate and flexible body bent forward like a lily in a storm.

"You never miss an opportunity to humiliate me in public," she said as several large teardrops rolled down her cheeks.

She dried her eyes in a theatrical gesture, then, with a melancholy smile directed at her fellow diners, murmured, "Excuse me," and rushed out of the room. Simona's gaze met that of the editorial director of the *Quotidiano delle Valli* and she remembered what he had said in the car about his potential desire to murder his wife.

Alberto Signorelli waited for the door to close behind her, then stood up and threw his napkin down on the table.

"Perhaps we should stop there," he said. "I have a collection of Armagnac and grappa in the parlor, and whoever is interested may enjoy a cigar. I have some Cohibas, Partagás, and El Rey del Monde Grandes de España."

As he was walking toward the parlor, the director of the *Quotidiano* took Giuseppe Felice by the shoulders— a picture that immediately recalled to Simona's mind the charming illustrations she'd seen in a children's book about bears and mice.

"Come on," he growled in his employee's ear, "don't make that face. You'll see; you'll have another shot at a big scoop very soon. Even sooner than you think."

"And it'll be too little, too late," the well-read Simona murmured to her husband.

* * *

When he had gone about half a mile in the larch forest, walking alongside the rocky precipices that jutted out over San Giorgio al Monte, Professor Martini set his backpack down on the ground and took a seat on a log to catch his breath. For several long minutes, with his eyes half-closed, he breathed in the air laden with the scent of tree sap. Then he leaned over, opened his backpack, and took out the camouflage jumpsuit and the disassembled Hecate II rifle. After changing out of his hiker's outfit and into his combatant's uniform, he began to assemble the gun before loading it with .500-caliber bullets, unaware that he was being discussed at the Signorelli castle at that very moment. Giuseppe Felice was saying that, according to some information he'd obtained through his friends at the International Association for the Study of Crime with contacts in the police force, Martini had served in the Bosnian army and had most likely even participated in the Siege of Sarajevo as a member of the defense forces.

"It doesn't take much to go from there to imagining him operating a sniper rifle," Simona noted, "and that's a connection Evangelisti and those in favor of the ecoterrorism theory wouldn't hesitate to make. I wouldn't be surprised if they found out that he'd been the one to establish a secret military faction within the Beekeepers' Defense League . . ."

"The usual Chartreuse for you?" Alberto asked Francesco.

After he'd filled his guests' glasses—a distillate of apple and chestnut for the commissario, a rue-infused Grappa della Serra for the police chief, a Janneau Trés Vieille Réserve Armagnac for Giuseppe Felice— he addressed his brother with that same tone of frank cordiality that he'd adopted since the evening began. Francesco at first had remained on the defensive, as though he wondered what cunning trick was hidden behind his older brother's about-face. But at a certain point, Alberto had alluded to the fact that Sacropiano might be interested in acquiring one of his agricultural estates in the vicinity of Ferrara, which produced pears and asparagus as its main crops and had been in deficit for three years. But its prospects were good, he promised, especially if a multinational corporation specializing in cutting-edge technologies like Sacropiano decided to take it under its wing.

"Of course you understand," the heavyset Alberto had said to the elegant Francesco, "it's not that I couldn't continue to absorb the losses myself for several years— the rest of my investments are fairly lucrative—but I don't have much time to devote to this particular property, so far from where most of my business is based. If I could just exchange a few words with the upper management at your company . . ."

Francesco assured him that he'd mention it the very next day, and that Sacropiano would surely take the *Quotidiano delle Valli*'s recent goodwill into consideration.

Simona had wondered, just for a second, if she and Marco wouldn't be better off leaving. Then her eyes had met the deflated gaze of Felice and she told herself that it would be too cruel to leave that little minnow alone with two big sharks. Moreover, it seemed to her that an air of theatricality reigned there that evening, and she wanted to see what would happen next. The scene of the wife's exit had kept Simona entertained for a bit, but now she was really starting to get bored. And so, as she always did in these situations, she drank. She was on her third glass. Marco kept giving her dirty looks. "You're driving anyway," she had muttered. Then Francesco Signorelli, who had drunk two large glasses of Chartreuse on the rocks, snorted:

"If the ecoterrorists were smart, they'd organize a little burglary here instead of taking on the center in Pinerolo."

"Hang on," Marco said, moving the bottle of liqueur on the low cashew-wood table out of his wife's reach, "wait a second. What do you mean by that?"

"There's a wing in this castle that belongs to me. My brother didn't tell you?"

"These matters are of little interest to our guests," Alberto Signorelli cut in, turning his glass of Bassano grappa, which he still hadn't drunk a drop of, around in his hands.

"But it is of interest to us," Francesco shot back with a grimace and a knowing look directed at his brother. "Especially as we wait for the details of our dearly departed parents' estate to be settled."

He seemed to feel that he had the upper hand as a result of Alberto's suggestion that Sacropiano buy his holding in Ferrara.

"At any rate, it's here in my study that they would find the documents with the results of the studies we conduct at the center to remedy colony collapse disorder. Documents that Bertolazzi had made unauthorized photocopies of and that the beekeepers were right on the verge of discovering at his home. But then he was killed and they cut the occupation short . . ."

"So in the end, Bertolazzi's murder occurred at just the right time," observed Felice.

Signorelli swiveled his head around to scrutinize the reporter's face with the expression of someone who had just noticed a cockroach crawling up a wall.

"What are you trying to insinuate?"

Felice raised his hands with his palms turned out.

"No, nothing, nothing at all."

Seeing as the executive's eyes continued to shoot daggers at the little redheaded man, Simona decided to divert his attention.

"So the secret of your investigation into Bertolazzi's murder can be found in the dossier in the prosecutor's possession?"

Francesco Signorelli shook his head.

"Oh, no. Evangelisti rightly felt that that information should remain the property of Sacropiano and returned the photocopies to me. They've joined the originals, and they're protected by this," he said, pulling out of his pocket a chain at the end of which dangled a round badge. "With this," he said, "we can get into the west wing of the castle and access my study. Second door on the right."

He nodded brusquely at the reporter.

"You'd like to rifle through my papers, wouldn't you, you dirty little communist? Always sticking your nose where it doesn't belong," he laid into Felice, who drew back in his chair.

"Oh, no . . . of course not . . ."

"Calm down," Alberto interjected. "Perhaps you've had a little too much to drink . . . You're clearly exhausted. You'd be better off if you stopped drinking for the night."

In fact, for a while now Francesco's eyelids had been coming to rest halfway over his eyes, and his speech had become labored.

"Don't get on my case," he muttered as he poured himself yet another glass of Chartreuse. "Are we out of ice?"

Alberto raised his fat carcass upright.

"I'll go look for some. No point calling our server. She'd take twenty minutes to bring it out of solidarity with her mistress."

He left the room. His brother stared at the glass, which he had filled halfway with Chartreuse.

"Eh," he said, "who gives a crap about the ice."

And he downed the glass. He closed his eyes. Two seconds later, the glass was rolling at his feet and he was snoring with his head leaning back on the headrest of the armchair, facing the ceiling.

Simona, Marco, and Felice exchanged glances. Then their eyes all jumped to the same object, as if drawn to it magnetically: the badge dangling at the end of the chain hanging from his pocket.

And it was in this position that Alberto Signorelli walked in on the three of them.

"My little brother has always been a teetotaler," he snorted.

Then he turned to Felice, towering over him like a mountain.

"And you, you son of a bitch, what's keeping you from doing your duty as a reporter? You have the chance to find out everything about the mysterious research conducted by Sacropiano and you're going to let it slip through your fingers? My brother's wing of the castle is right behind that door," he added, pointing to an ornate double door decorated with carved circular windows and pastoral scenes. "Third door on the right, at the end of the hall. The study is in the tower; you take the elevator to get to it."

From deep in his seat, Felice shook his head.

"I don't know . . . I don't think I can do it . . ."

Alberto Signorelli rolled his bulging eyes.

"You imbecile! Don't you realize that you don't have a choice? You want to lose your job? If I go, it will be a betrayal of familial trust. But you, you would only be practicing your profession . . ."

At every one of his boss's points, Felice shook his head violently.

Simona leapt up from her armchair, took the badge, and made a beeline for the indicated door.

"Come on, Felice!" she called out.

"Simona," Marco shouted, "get back here! You're crazy!"

With her hand on one of the double doors, she turned around to face her husband.

"That's why you love me, isn't it? Let's go!" she shouted at the reporter. "Do as I say. That's a police order! Hurry, before he wakes up!"

Alberto drew near her and said under his breath, "Don't worry about that. With what I put in his Chartreuse, he's going to be out for a good while. This pig really thinks that I don't give a crap about my property in Ferrara? Let's go, Felice," he added, swiveling around on his heels and turning his scorching glare on his employee. "To work! I only said that Item Number 78C is a detail, not that I wanted to let it go. When I went to get the ice, I was detained by a phone call in the next room over, and you took advantage of my absence to gather some information. What could be more natural, right?"

* * *

In the meantime, the elegant bald man whose balls the commissario had busted in the elevator was on the phone with the magistrate.

"Dottore, I'm sorry to disturb you at home at this late hour, but it's very urgent. The surveillance service just conveyed to me an email sent to Commissario Tavianello by Professor Martini. As far as we can tell she hasn't viewed this message yet. Right now she's at dinner at the Signorelli castle . . . Yes, we have our sources. Shall I read you the email? It seems to me it could mean trouble . . . All right then:

Dear Simona,

I take the liberty of calling you by name because I got the impression that you were one of the few people I'd met in recent years who more or less understood what was on the verge of happening. I have a confession to make, in order to keep the poor beekeepers in the Defense League from rotting in prison. I was the one who shot Mauro Danela, the madman who criticized Minoncelli for introducing foreign bees into Italian territory. I was also the one who shot Berisha. Since the years of the Siege of Sarajevo, a time when I was as invested in the fate of my fellow human beings as I was in the fate of the bees (I have changed quite a lot since then in this respect), I've owned a copolymer Hecate II rifle with a Scrome J10 10x40 scope with a Mil-Dot reticle on a NATO/STANAG rail, which shoots .500-caliber bullets. It was given to me during the Yugoslav Wars by a Bosnian friend of mine who had stolen it from a Serb; I will spare you the details.

In fact, for a period of several months, I played the part of the guerilla fighter, just for fun. I donned a military jumpsuit and amused myself by capturing various people in my crosshairs from the edges of the forest, but it never would have occurred to me to actually *shoot* anyone. But when I took it out of the shed in my garden, where it had been lying in wait patiently for fourteen years, my only intention was to defend a certain part of the mountain, to which Mehmet Berisha had the bad judgment to wander too close. But that happened purely by chance, and I only managed to hit his leg. However, I confess that I lost my cool when I saw that idiot Danela destroy Minoncelli's apiary. I had been watching our friend's house for a while because I had noticed that he'd been having a lot of visitors. I have a sneaking suspicion that our famous Services—the envy of the entire world—sent several agents here to keep an eye on things, with the goal of protecting the experiments being conducted in Pinerolo by the Doctor Strangeloves of the biosphere. I confess that I wouldn't have minded taking out one or two of them . . .

Evangelisti's interlocutor stopped reading.

"Fuck! Do you realize what that means? The bastard was this close to shooting me!"

"Go on," said the magistrate, as he zipped up his fly and flushed. "Keep reading this interesting email," he insisted, closing the bathroom door behind him and casting a melancholy glance at the large cup of gelato on the kitchen table. It was melting rapidly.

"All right then, I'll keep going: '. . . taking out one or two of them. But none of that matters now, since the first phase of The Worker Bee Revolution is nearly complete. After the exile, the return.' That's it."

"What do you mean, 'That's it'?"

"That's it. That's how it ends: 'After the exile, the return.'"

"I'll call Calabonda right away, and DIGOS. I need to get my hands on Martini so that he can explain these obscure passages."

"And the guys from the Defense League? What are you going to do with them? You really think they were involved in the failed attack?"

"Ah, we'll see about that. We have time to figure it out. Justice will have its day, you know."

The other man snorted. "In the Services, we're paid to know that. Literally. At least we have been since the Piazza Fontana bombing in '69!"

Evangelisti got off the phone as fast as he could to make the necessary calls. If he was quick and to the point, maybe the gelato wouldn't melt too much.

* * *

From that enormous balcony overlooking the Alps, on the stone-strewn terrain out of which jutted black, oblong rocks, humanity's lights down below seemed dim compared to the thousands of stars whose light reached Earth after traveling the immense silence of infinite space, very often long after their originators had died. In the darkness, Martini removed his military jumpsuit and, completely naked, pulled a large metal drum from a carefully camouflaged hiding place at the foot of a rock. His panting from the arduous climb hadn't abated, but he was now eager to get it over with. He removed the cap, lifted the heavy container in his arms, and the sweet mixture he'd concocted to nourish his revolutionary friends began to pour over his body. He sang softly:

> You flew far from our trees
> my golden bees,
> along exile's path
> to escape the wrath
> of capitalist life,
> but now you must return,
> it's time to say enough,
> enough apologies
> from supertechnologies,
> enough nanoparticles,
> no more bits and megabytes,
> enough chips and GMOs,
> enough with pesticides
> and all the world's genocides.

With his body sticky, swaying, panting, he reached the edge of the precipice that delimited the relatively flat expanse. There, at the foot of a black rock, two steps from the precipice, was a gap in the stone. Kneeling down, he heard the sound. It was the entrance to a cave that must have been very deep and very wide, because the buzzing that rose up to his ears thundered like the rumbling of a mountain-sized giant's uvula.

A bee came to rest on Aldo Martini's forehead, another at the corner of his mouth. A third on his right hand. A fourth, a fifth . . .

The buzzing grew louder.

"You're here," he said, "you're all here. All the ones that left the apiaries in the valley."

Now his entire face, his neck, and his shoulders were covered with teeming, loudly buzzing bees.

His lips, with dozens of legs moving all over them, articulated the words:

"There are millions of you, and you will return."

* * *

"So, that's what it is?" Simona said. "This is Sacropiano's project?"

Sunk into the armchair in Francesco's study in the west tower, part of an addition built in the nineteenth century, the commissario shook her head incredulously. Giuseppe Felice stared at the screen occupied in its entirety by the image of a bluish rectangle and murmured:

"That's it. Replacing the bees. With self-replicating nanorobots . . ."

He clicked on an icon at the bottom of the screen, opened a document, and read out loud for the third time:

> ... smaller than a grain of pollen, but capable of transporting them, they should prove to be infinitely more productive in terms of fertilization, and, therefore, infinitely lucrative. In the past, bees performed a job that remained firmly in the sphere of free labor: who could know how many bees from a given apiary it had taken to fertilize a single wild plant? Impossible. With our fertilizing nanorobots, our venture could allow us to extract a fee for every plant on earth fertilized by them. In a certain sense, this will mean the end of wild vegetation as we know it, as soon as we assume control of the reproduction of the majority of the world's plants ...

"Incredible," said Marco, darting a worried look down the hall from his place in the doorway. "Now, shall we go?"

"It's always the same process," Felice observed. "Something that exists in nature and is available for free is destroyed and replaced by an artificial prosthesis that has to be paid for."

"Shall we go?" Marco repeated.

Simona got to her feet. The liqueur she'd drunk was beginning to have undesirable secondary effects on her.

"Let's go," she said. "Let's go. But where?"

*   *   *

Quotidiano delle Valli

Incredible Attempted Suicide Attack on the Pinerolo Research Center.

Behind the wheel of a stolen tractor, Professor Martini of San Giorgio al Monte plowed down the fence and the gates of the center before setting himself on fire. According to numerous witnesses, the tractor was followed by a "giant swarm of millions of bees." The swarm reportedly disappeared minutes after the fire began.

Psychiatrists believe this to have been a "collective hallucination revealing unconscious fears." The professor's body was later identified.

It was an unprecedented event that seems to have taken place right in our quiet little valley . . . (Giuseppe Felice's article continues on page 2, along with Bruno Ciuffani's claims of "bias on the part of Commissario Tavianello, who persistently encouraged the disregard for democratic institutions.")

* * *

Simona was always the one to drive. As usual, she had plonked her shapeless purse in her husband's lap, but Marco didn't even notice; he was too absorbed in skimming the newspaper's headlines. He flipped through it nervously, turning the page again and again and again.

"Unbelievable," he said finally. "There isn't a single word about the Sacropiano project!"

"I guess that Alberto Signorelli decided to use it to put pressure on his brother and on Sacropiano. What a twisted relationship."

"At any rate, the world should know . . ." Marco began.

"About the self-replicating nanorobots that would take the place of bees? But it's science fiction nonsense!"

"What are you talking about?" said the police chief as he threw the purse in the backseat.

"I'll tell you what they'll say if we tell them about it . . . What time do you think we'll get to Turin?"

"Who cares? We have all the time in the world, don't we? Is that all you have to say about it? You think that the fact that Sacropiano's research center has been destroyed will stop them? To the contrary, now that they can pose as victims of ecoterrorism, I think they'll be able to accelerate . . ."

"Or maybe we can find an Internet café before we get to Turin," said Simona, who seemed to be following her own line of thought without paying much attention to what her husband was saying. "Pay attention to the cities we're going past."

"An Internet café? What for?"

"Because I don't know whether I'll be able to send such a large file from my computer if I'm connected to my mobile network . . ."

"What file? Wait . . . did you . . ."

"Well, yes. There was a flash drive in one of Signorelli's desk drawers. I have a copy of it too. And unlike Felice,

I don't have bosses who would keep me from making it public."

"Simona, you're . . . you're . . ."

"Yes, I know. Would you light a cigarette and pass it to me? I think I'm ready to start smoking again."

*   *   *

When she had extinguished the cigarette and the maps showed that they were approaching Turin, she asked, "Do you think they'll come back?"

"Who?"

"The bees. The millions of bees that were following Martini."

"Simona, you know that was a collective hallucination."

"Ah, no. I don't know that at all."

*   *   *

A little later, when they had just parked outside an Internet café, she returned to the subject.

"Let's say that it wasn't a hallucination. Do you think they'll come back? All of the bees that disappeared—and not just from the valley. And if they do come back, what will they do?"

"Who knows?" Marco said. "Who knows?"

A note on titles and roles in the book:

In Italy, a commissario is responsible for leading criminal investigations and various other police operations. In keeping with convention, Simona Tavianello's title has been left untranslated. Marco Tavianello's title is "capo commissario" in Italian, translated here as "police chief."

The Carabinieri, a law enforcement unit that is actually a branch of the military, are led locally by the maresciallo. Because this title has no clear equivalent in the American military, Calabonda's title is left untranslated here. It is also worth noting that Carabinieri are conceived of as oafish and stupid by the national imagination, and are the frequent butts of jokes.